For June and John,
with love and thanks.

OXFORD
UNIVERSITY PRESS

Great Clarendon Street, Oxford, OX2 6DP,
United Kingdom

Oxford University Press is a department of the University of Oxford.
It furthers the University's objective of excellence in research, scholarship,
and education by publishing worldwide. Oxford is a registered trade mark of
Oxford University Press in the UK and in certain other countries

Text and illustrations © Dave Cousins 2015

First published in 2015

This book is a work of fiction. Names, characters, businesses, organizations, places,
and events are either the product of the author's imagination, or are used
fictitiously. Any resemblance to actual persons, living or dead, events or locales,
is entirely coincidental.

British Library Cataloguing in Publication Data

ISBN: 978-0-19-2738233

1 3 5 7 9 10 8 6 4 2

Printed in Great Britain by CPI Group UK Ltd, Croydon, CR0 4YY

Paper used in the production of this book is a natural,
recyclable product made from wood grown in sustainable forests.
The manufacturing process conforms to the environmental
regulations of the country of origin.

Name:

Name:

CHARLIE MERRICK

Squad:

MISFITS

HELP!

Somebody get me out of here!
This is all a HUGE MISTAKE!
I can't believe we ended up in this mess!
Or can I? Now I think about it, this is EXACTLY
the kind of thing that ALWAYS happens to us!
Though I have to say that this one takes things to
a whole new level on the EPIC DISASTER SCALE.

I've just been given this NOTEBOOK. We're supposed to keep a diary of our week here at the camp—make notes about the things we learn—write down our feelings, that kind of stuff. My best mate Sam chucked his on the bonfire when nobody was looking, but here I am using mine already.

Last year I kept a record of our football team's entire season. I'm surprised how much I've missed doing it, so I'm thinking if I write down everything that happens here, maybe one day I'll be able to look back at it and LAUGH . . . ONE DAY.

I should probably start by explaining how I ended up here.

To begin with, we were LATE. Had I known then what I know now, I wouldn't have told Sam to start running . . .

ME

SAM →

1

ALL
ABOARD
THE
FRANKENBUS!

07:54—UNDIES FROM HEAVEN

'SAM! Come ON! We're going to miss the bus!'

We'd only run to the end of the road, but Sam was already out of breath from dragging the giant suitcase on wheels he'd borrowed from his mum.

'It's this case,' he said. 'It's not built for speed!'

I checked my watch—we couldn't be late—not today! The entire summer had been leading up to this—no way was I going to miss it.

'SHORTCUT!' I said, darting down a path between two houses.

'Charlie! Where are you going?' I could hear Sam behind me, crashing his way through the wheelie bins lining the narrow alley.

'Trust me,' I shouted, jogging past a line of garages, then down some steps into the underpass. A minute later we came out onto the long straight road leading to Northfield Park.

'You're a genius!' said Sam. 'We're almost there!'

'Yeah, but we're still late. Come on!'

'Doug wouldn't go without us,' said Sam. 'Would he?'
We both knew the answer to that.

Sam set off up the road like his shorts were on fire, the case swerving and bouncing after him.

There was a bloke walking his dog coming the other way, and Sam dodged to avoid them—which is when it happened.

Having been pushed beyond their limits for the entire frantic journey, the tiny wheels on the case decided they'd had enough—and disintegrated.

The case flipped . . . bounced . . . then slammed into a lamp post.

The impact blew the lid open as effectively as dynamite, blasting all of Sam's stuff into the air. Socks, pants, T-shirts, and football boots rained down, clattering across the pavement and into the road.

For a moment we didn't move, just stared in disbelief at the devastation. Then I remembered we had a bus to catch.

'Quick! Grab your stuff and shove it back in!'
'The lid's smashed,' said Sam. 'It won't stay shut!'

I took off my football scarf and tied it around the case. 'That should hold it for now,' I said. 'Let's go!'

But Sam didn't move. He was staring over my shoulder up the road.

I turned . . . and saw a silver coach pulling out of the car park.

'NOOOOOOOOOOO!'

I dropped my bag and ran, waving my arms and shouting—but I was too late, too far away.

All I could do was watch, as the coach, and our week at football camp disappeared into the distance.

11

'They left us behind!' said Sam. 'After all that!'

I sat down on the pavement staring at the empty space where the coach had been.

THEY'D ACTUALLY GONE WITHOUT US!

Or had they . . .

I stood up. 'Wait a minute—what's that?'

'What?' Sam squinted up the road.

I pointed. 'THAT!'

I'd been so busy chasing the big silver coach, I hadn't noticed the minibus waiting in the car park.

'What happened to you two?' said Jasmine, as we ran through the gate.

'Long story,' I said, gasping for breath.

She rolled her eyes. 'Isn't it always with you?'

'This way for the SOCCER CAMP SPECIAL,' said Gerbil, sweeping an arm towards the minibus.

'Where did THAT come from?'

'It's our new team bus,' said Donut.

'NEW?' Sam frowned. 'It looks like someone took three wrecked vans and tried to build one good one from all the bits.'

'And failed!' muttered Jasmine.

'Like Frankenstein's Monster!' I laughed. 'Hey! We should call it the FRANKENBUS!'

'No we shouldn't,' said Doug, looking hurt. 'Now sling your stuff in and get on board—we've got a long journey ahead and we're already late.'

Just in case you're sitting there thinking—DONUT? GERBIL? Is he REALLY having a conversation with a cake and a talking rodent? I should probably explain...

Everyone on board the Frankenbus is part of North Star Galaxy Under-12s football team—and once you get a nickname, you're stuck with it.

(BACK ROW) DOUG (MANAGER), NATHAN, MOLE*, KASH, DONUT, LUKAS*
(FRONT ROW) OSCAR, SAM, CHARLIE (ME!), GERBIL, MIKO*
JAS ISN'T IN THE PICTURE BECAUSE SHE ONLY JOINED AFTER THE LEAGUE ANNOUNCED MIXED TEAMS WOULD BE ALLOWED NEXT SEASON.
(*THESE PLAYERS COULDN'T COME WITH US TO TRAINING CAMP)

Gerbil's really called CIARAN, and Donut is actually Duncan—DUNCAN DONUT—get it?

Sam and Jasmine are my two best mates. We met on the first day in Reception—me and Sam were fighting over a football, and Jas stepped in to break it up! We've been together ever since.

ME, SAM AND JAS AT SAM'S 5TH BIRTHDAY PARTY

13:13—
A MIGHTY-B & FRiES TO GO

The Frankenbus belched a cloud of blue smoke across the service-station car park, and spluttered to a halt.

'Right, I want everyone back in twenty minutes,' Doug called after us, as we poured out of the bus.

'Hey! There's some grass over there,' said Oscar. 'Anyone fancy a kick about?'

Sam shook his head. 'FOOD! I need food—fast.'

'How can you be hungry?' said Jasmine. 'You've been stuffing your face all the way here!'

'Gotta keep my strength up,' said Sam, pushing open the doors. 'YES! They've got a MIGHTY-B!'

Sam shot towards the burger bar like he'd been caught in a tractor beam.

'The last time I had a MIGHTY-B Cola, I gave my Gran some,' said Gerbil. 'She did this massive burp and shot her false teeth out!'

'You're making that up,' said Jas.

Gerbil grimaced. 'I wish! They landed in my chips!'

'That is so gross!'
Jasmine pulled a face.
'I'm beginning to think
coming on this trip was
a bad idea. A week at
a football camp in France
would have been worth
putting up with you lot, but now . . .'

OOOPS! WAS THAT ME?

Gerbil frowned. 'I never quite
understood why we couldn't go
to France. What happened?'

'Well . . . Doug was involved, so it's complicated
and shrouded in mystery!' I told him. 'Donut said it
was something to do with Doug not being welcome
across the border, after an incident involving the
police, a pair of circus clowns, and a lorry load of
cheese—apparently.'

Gerbil sighed. 'Yeah, that sounds like Doug!'

17

Twenty minutes later we were back in the bus. I held my breath as Doug inserted the key to start the engine—certain it wouldn't work. We'd be stuck for hours waiting for a recovery truck and never make it to the football camp. It's the kind of thing that ALWAYS happens to us.

But the Frankenbus burst into life, firing off a sound like a gunshot. A bloke walking past dropped his burger in fear—but we were already making our escape in a concealing cloud of blue smoke.

My best friends in the whole world were in this bus—CHARLIE MERRICK'S MISFITS—that's what Sam called us when I got everyone together. It was

WAIT!

GRRRRRR

HONK!!

IJ DAVIES & SON
BUILDING CONTRACTORS

a good name for a bunch of players that nobody else wanted. We weren't the best footballers, but over the course of a season we learned to play as a team. To everyone else we still look like misfits, but for us, this is EXACTLY where we BELONG.

It was a shame Lukas, Mole and Miko couldn't come, but apart from those three, we were all here.

So why was there a spare seat?

The Frankenbus was gathering speed, heading for the ramp back onto the motorway.

I was sure the van had been full when we set out.

Then I realized—

STOP!

WE'VE LEFT DONUT BEHIND!

SCREECH!

MOTORWAY

22:17—ARE WE THERE YET?

It felt like we'd been driving for hours through an endless forest of dark trees.

'We're going to run out of petrol soon,' said Donut. 'We'll be stranded—in the middle of nowhere!'

'With no food!' Sam sounded worried.

Jasmine grinned. 'They'll find the Frankenbus weeks later—empty, except for Sam and a pile of our bones, all licked clean and shiny!'

We were still arguing over who Sam would eat first, when Doug finally turned off the main road.

Branches clawed at the bus as we bumped along a narrow track.

'Strange place for a football camp,' said Oscar.

Jas peered into the darkness. 'This is creepy.'

'I can't see any goalposts,' said Sam. 'Or pitches.'

'Maybe it's deliberate,' said Gerbil. 'Like a secret training base!'

Then we saw a building up ahead. Lights shone in the windows and there were vehicles parked outside.

As we swung into the car park the headlights flashed across a shiny black minibus.

'The Wild Warriors,' said Jasmine, reading the writing on the side.

'Must be one of the other teams,' I said, feeling a tingle of anticipation in my guts.

The Frankenbus announced our arrival with a loud bang. Moments later a man emerged from the building. He was dressed in camouflage shorts and vest, and had tattoos covering his shoulders and arms.

Doug wound down his window and the man's face peered in at us.

'Get a bit lost did you?' He smiled and thrust a meaty arm through the space to shake hands with Doug. I noticed one of his fingers was missing.

'I'm Clive,' he said. 'Folks here call me Survival Clive!' Then he laughed.

It was hard to be sure in the dark, but it looked like Clive had a serious scar down one side of his face and . . .

'Is that a glass eye?' said Sam, in a loud whisper.

'Well spotted,' said Survival Clive, winking his good eye at Sam. 'I'll tell you how I lost it sometime.'

Survival Clive didn't look much like a football coach—though it was hard to tell in the dark. Maybe he'd been a centre-half? A lot of defenders looked like boxers after a few seasons . . . but losing an eye and a finger—that was extreme! Perhaps that was where the weird nickname came from.

'Right,' he said. 'Let's get you guys unloaded.'

We climbed out of the Frankenbus and grabbed our stuff.

'Not sure you'll be needing those!' said Survival Clive, when Doug picked up the bag of footballs.

'Oh, right,' said Doug. 'You provide them do you?'

Clive frowned. 'Why would we provide footballs?'

'For training.'

For a moment Survival Clive seemed confused, then he laughed and slapped Doug on the shoulder like he'd made a great joke.

'This isn't a football training camp, mate!'

'It isn't?'

We stopped unloading and stared at him.

'What do you mean, NOT a football camp?' I said.

24

Survival Clive looked at me. 'This is the GO! WILD
Survival Centre. Bushcraft and wilderness training!'
    I'm not sure what my face looked like at that
moment, but I'm guessing it was probably something
like this—

2

STAYING ALIVE

WITH
SURVIVAL
CLIVE

06:03—THE WALL OF THE WILD

WHO GETS UP THIS EARLY?!!

After spending the night on creaking bunk beds in a spooky old barn, we stumbled bleary-eyed into the Go! Wild Centre in search of breakfast.

'I can't believe Doug booked the wrong course!' said Jasmine.

'Apparently SOCCER and SURVIVAL were next to each other on the website,' I said. 'He's sorting out a transfer to the football camp this morning.'

'Good!' said Sam. 'This place is weird.' He stopped in front of a giant noticeboard headed: THE WALL OF THE WILD. 'Is that meant to be a JOKE?'

The board was covered with photographs of kids in the woods, carrying piles of sticks, or grinning round bonfires. Jasmine pointed to one.

'Hey! This says it's the Wild Warriors. Wasn't their van parked outside last night?'

27

SURVIVAL CHALLENGE WINNERS:
WILD WARRIORS Falcon, Owl, Hawk, Kestrel

'What kind of a stupid name is Owl?' said Gerbil.

Jas raised an eyebrow.

'What?' said Gerbil.

Then the door opened, and the Wild Warriors themselves burst in. They were dressed in camouflage gear. The girl in front was carrying a large stick and wearing a furry animal hat—a grey wolf with yellow eyes and a fringe of plastic teeth. On anyone else it might have looked cute—on her it looked like a hunting trophy.

She scowled at us.

'What are YOU looking at?'

'We saw your picture on the wall,' said Jas.

A girl with glasses and wiry orange hair stepped forward. 'Actually Magpie wasn't with us last time,' she said. 'I'm Owl—Wild Warriors squad leader—last year's winners.'

Wolf Hat Girl, AKA Magpie, pointed at my blue and yellow North Star Galaxy tracksuit. 'Why are you all dressed like that?'

'We're a football team,' I said.

'A FOOTBALL team!' She snorted. 'I hate football.'

The other girls sniggered.

'So what are you doing HERE?' asked Owl.

'It's a long story,' Jas said. 'But we're not staying.'

'Just as well.' Owl swept her eyes over us. 'The Go! Wild Survival Challenge is tough. I'm not sure YOU'D be up to it.'

I was about to ask exactly what she meant by that, when Doug appeared.

'So, can we go now?' said Sam.

'Um . . . about that.' Doug frowned. 'It seems the football course is all booked up now. I tried a couple of others, but they can't take us either.' He tugged his beard. 'It's too late to get a refund, so . . . I was thinking . . . we might as well stay here.'

07:32—GO! WILD TRAINING HALL

(AKA another old barn!)

'I don't believe we're stuck here!' said Sam, slumping onto the bench next to me. 'We should be playing football now, not learning survival skills from a bloke with one eye and a missing finger!'

'I wonder what happened to his eye?' whispered Gerbil.

'Ask him,' said Sam.

'YOU ask him!' said Gerbil.

Then they both looked at me.

'No way!' I said, as Survival Clive clapped his hands and called for quiet.

'I hope you all had a good breakfast,' he said, 'because from now on, you will be eating only what you can catch and kill for yourselves.'

'WHAT?!' said Sam.

Survival Clive grinned. 'I'm joking . . . but what if I wasn't? Imagine these buildings burned down. We'd be left with nothing but the clothes we are wearing and whatever we have in our pockets.' He paused. 'I want each of you to imagine what that would be like. What would you do next? How long could YOU survive?'

I'VE GOT MY EYE ON YOU . . .

'I'd jump in the Frankenbus and get out of here,' muttered Gerbil.

Survival Clive heard him. 'No good! The vehicles were destroyed in the fire. The only way out of here is on foot. And just in case you were wondering, the nearest town is a two-day hike in that direction.' He pointed towards the dense forest surrounding us on all sides.

'I'd phone my dad and get him to pick us up,' said one of the Wild Warriors.

Survival Clive shook his head again. 'I'm sure most of you will have already discovered that we have no mobile reception here, and the landline just got fried in the fire. Calling for help is not an option.' He smiled. 'Of course, you could simply wait to be rescued. I'm sure somebody would come looking for us when you failed to return home at the end of the week. But that's six days away. In the meantime you're going to need water, food and shelter to stay alive.'

Survival Clive paused, and his words hung in the dusty air.

'The world we live in allows us to take these things for granted,' he continued. 'We get thirsty, and all we have to do is turn on a tap. Heat is pumped round our homes in radiators; our fridges are full of food. But these things are fragile—they could be taken away like that!' He snapped his fingers and Gerbil jumped. 'This week will teach you some of the skills you'll need to survive without these modern luxuries—skills our ancestors would have known as a way of life.'

Survival Clive picked up a pile of notebooks and handed them out.

'These are for you to record your week here with us, the things you learn—not just new skills, but about yourselves too.'

'Great!' said Sam. 'A workbook! I bet we wouldn't have had to do writing at football camp.'

THE ONE i'M WRITING iN NOW!

HOW TO MAKE A PAPER CUP

SURVIVAL TIP

Use this cup to carry foraged fruit or water for drinking. All you need is a single sheet of paper. Strong, shiny paper (the kind used for magazines and leaflets) is best for holding liquids.*

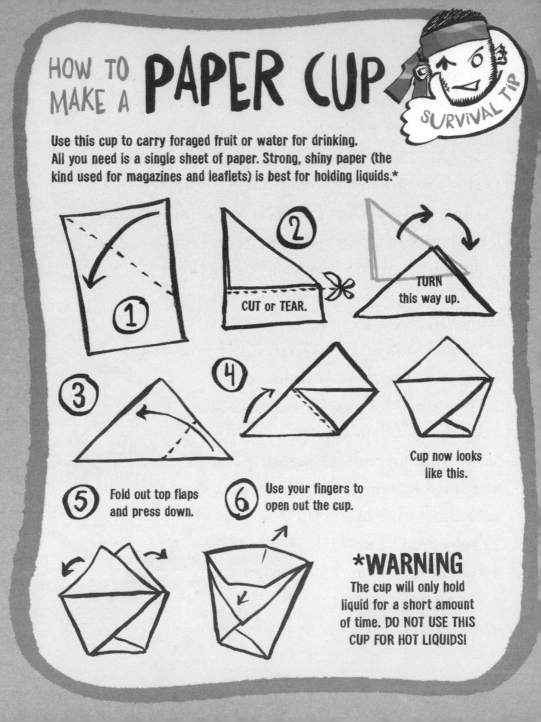

①

② CUT or TEAR.

TURN this way up.

③

④ Cup now looks like this.

⑤ Fold out top flaps and press down.

⑥ Use your fingers to open out the cup.

*WARNING
The cup will only hold liquid for a short amount of time. DO NOT USE THIS CUP FOR HOT LIQUIDS!

← 'Look, it's got survival tips,' said Gerbil, flicking through the pages. 'How to make a paper cup from a single sheet of paper!'

Sam snorted. 'Like that's gonna work!'

(I made one and it really did!)

Next, Survival Clive split us into four 'squads', and gave us five minutes to come up with a name.

Sam wanted KILL SQUAD ALPHA.

'We're only going camping in the woods,' I said, 'not a black ops mission.'

'How about THE LOST BOYS?' suggested Gerbil.

Jasmine raised her eyebrows. 'Er, hello!'

'Why don't we just be the MISFITS?' I said.

We hadn't come up with anything better when Survival Clive called time, so MISFITS it was. Sam was furious when he saw that Oscar's squad was called the FOREST FREAKS.

'Why didn't we think of that?' he hissed. 'That name is so much better than ours!'

Magpie's squad kept the WILD WARRIORS name, while the rest of their group became the FIREFLIES.

Name: CHARLIE MERRICK
Skills: DETERMINATION & DRAWING.
(ALL THE 'D'S—WELL TWO ANYWAY.)
WILD FACT: NOT REALLY INTO THE WILD, BUT IF WINNING THIS SHUTS MAGPIE UP, SHOW ME THE FOREST & LET'S GO!

CHARLIE

Name: JASMINE LAWRENCE
Skills: NO FEAR.
ALSO GOOD AT GETTING OTHER PEOPLE TO CARRY HER STUFF.
WILD FACT: JAS IS SECRETLY QUITE HAPPY TO HAVE A FEW DAYS CAMPING IN THE SUN.

JASMINE

SAM

Name: SAMSON CHARSLEY
Skills: EATING—HE NEVER STOPS OR GETS FULL.
(MUST HAVE HOLLOW LEGS!)
WILD FACT: SAM IS SCARED OF WATER . . . AND HEIGHTS!

Name: CIARAN MORGAN.
Skills: SINGING!
WILD FACT: WHEN HE WAS SMALL(ER) GERBIL LOVED TARZAN & SPENT ALL HIS TIME JUMPING OFF HIS BED WEARING LEOPARD PRINT TRUNKS GOING "AAAAAHHHAAAH!"

GERBIL

MISFITS

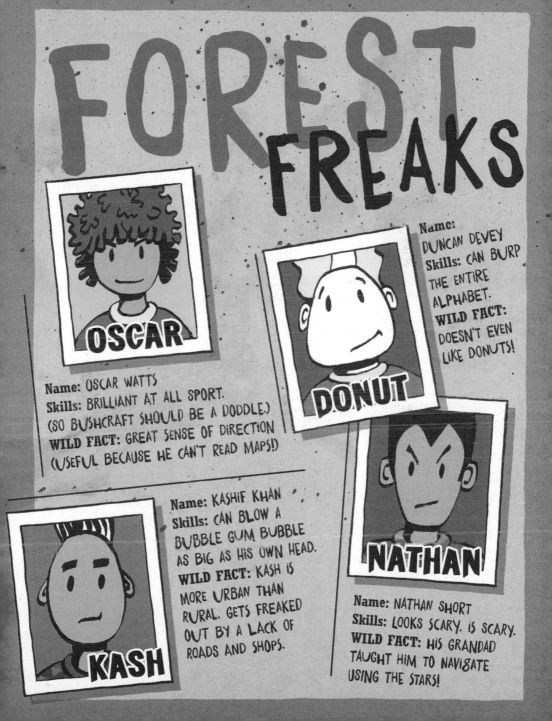

FIREFLIES

Name: MARTHA DURRANT
Skills: EXPLOSIVE ORIGAMI EXPERT.
WILD FACT: WORLD RECORD HOLDER FOR JELLY JUGGLING.

EAGLE

Name: SCARLET BOUVIER
Skills: FLUENT AT SPEAKING BACKWARDS. SADLY NOBODY ELSE UNDERSTANDS A WORD!
WILD FACT: SLEEPS IN A TREEHOUSE AND WAS RAISED BY A FAMILY OF WILD WOLVES.

RED KITE

HARRIER

Name: SYDNEY HARPER
Skills: MUSHROOM HUNTING.
WILD FACT: JUNIOR TROUT TICKLING CHAMPION FOR THREE YEARS RUNNING.

Name: CHITRA DEVI
Skills: PART GIRL— PART DOLPHIN. CAN STAY UNDERWATER FOR AGES.
WILD FACT: SCARED OF THE DARK AND ALWAYS TAKES EIGHT TORCHES TO BED.

CONDOR

'For the next two days my team will teach you the basic skills you will need to survive in the WILD,' said Survival Clive. 'Squads will earn points based on how well they perform each training task. There will be more points at stake once you Go! Wild, and have to survive for four days in the forest. The squad with the highest score at the end of the week will earn themselves a place on the WALL OF THE WILD!'

'Do we get a trophy?' said Sam.

Survival Clive laughed and shook his head.

Magpie snorted. 'I wouldn't worry about it, Football Boy,' she said. 'You won't win anyway.'

Sam shrugged. 'Hardly seems worth the effort if there's no cup.'

But from the moment Survival Clive had mentioned teams and points, I'd felt the familiar tingle in the hairs at the back of my neck. Maybe it was seeing our name on the leader board, or the way the Wild Warriors had dismissed our chances. Just because we looked like we didn't belong on the WALL OF THE WILD, didn't mean we COULDN'T win.

GO! WILD
STAFF PROFILE

COWBOY HAT

PONYTAIL!!!

I THINK THAT'S SUPPOSED TO BE A BEARD!

DOG TAGS

TARPAULIN

PARACORD

OUTBACK

19 YEARS OLD. WORKING THE COWBOY SURFER DUDE LOOK. CALLED OUTBACK BECAUSE HE NEVER STOPS TALKING (IN A FAKE AUSSIE ACCENT) ABOUT THE ONE WEEK HE SPENT WILD CAMPING IN THE AUSTRALIAN OUTBACK!

FLIP-FLOPS!

10:30—GO! WiLD WOODLAND TRAINING AREA

Squads trained in pairs. For the first session we were with the Fireflies, while Oscar's Forest Freaks trained alongside the Wild Warriors.

'One of the most important survival skills,' said Outback, 'is knowing how to build a shelter. Personally, I like to use what nature provides—but that takes time and skill. If you need to get yourself under cover quick, this HERE is your best friend.'

He held up a folded square of blue plastic.

'This is a tarpaulin—or TARP—as we call it in the bush. I've used these beauties to carry firewood, collect water—even waterproof a boat! This morning I'm going to show you how to make a quick, adjustable, waterproof shelter from a tarp and a few metres of paracord rope.'

Outback picked up a watering can and grinned.

'Then, just to make sure your shelters are up to the job, we're going to make it RAIN!'

Outback demonstrated how to rig a tarp shelter between two trees, then split us into pairs to make our own.

It looked easy enough. Me and Jasmine tied the cord round one trunk without any problem, but then we couldn't get the second fixing to work. The knot was supposed to slide and tighten the line, but ours wouldn't move, so the tarp sagged like a pair of giant blue underpants on a washing line.

Jas frowned. 'Maybe we should start again.'

I looked round at the others—both Firefly pairs had almost finished—even Sam and Gerbil's shelter was taking shape.

'Three more minutes guys,' Outback called out. 'I sense a storm brewing!'

'No time,' I said. 'If we peg the corners out, it might be OK.'

Jas tied the paracord to the tarp, while I found some sticks to use as pegs, hammering them into the ground with a thick length of branch. The problem came when we tried to get the lines to tighten.

'We need that funny knot again,' said Jas.

'Fifteen seconds,' said Outback.

'Just bodge it!' I said, desperately winding the cord around the pegs.

Outback picked up the watering can. 'Here comes the rain!'

Sam and Gerbil slid under their tarp as the water rattled down, splashing over the sides. Sam pulled his feet in, then started to laugh. All around them the ground was wet, but under the shelter it was completely dry.

Outback grinned. 'Good work, guys!' he said. 'That's two points on the board for the Misfits.'

Of course the Firefly shelters were perfect.

Then it was our turn.

Me and Jas huddled together under our sagging tarpaulin, while the watering can rainstorm crashed over us. Jasmine yelped as water trickled down her back—then the main line slipped from our failed knot . . . and the whole lot came down.

HOW TO BUILD A TARP SHELTER

① Find two trees slightly further apart than the length of your tarpaulin.

② Tie a length of CORD between the trees (at shoulder height) to form a ridge line. Use a BOWLINE KNOT* at the first tree, and a TAUTLINE HITCH for the second. The Tautline Hitch knot will slide to keep the ridge line taut.

* See following page for OUTBACK'S HANDY GUIDE to KNOTS!

③ Tie lengths of cord to the holes at each corner of your TARPAULIN with a BOWLINE KNOT.

(4) Hang the TARPAULIN over the ridge line and adjust the TAUTLINE HITCH knot so the shelter doesn't sag.

(5) Open the tarpaulin and peg out the corner lines. Attach to pegs** with TAUTLINE HITCH KNOTS.

** TIP—Make pegs from branches. Use a rock or thick log as a hammer.

SURVIVAL TIP

OUTBACK'S HANDY GUIDE

#1—THE BOWLINE

An easy way to remember how to tie a BOWLINE is this: imagine the end of the cord is a rabbit! (1) The rabbit goes around the tree, (2) out up through the hole (3) under the line, then (4) back down the hole. (5) To finish off, give his ears a tug to tighten the knot! *NOTE—Do not try this with a real rabbit!

TO KNOTS

#2—THE TAUTLINE HITCH

(1) Loop the cord around the tree, then back OVER itself.
(2) Loop OVER a second time, then (3) UP through the loop.
(4) Now take the end of the cord UNDER the main part of the line
(5) then DOWN through the loop and out. (6) The finished knot will
now slide up and down to keep the line taut.

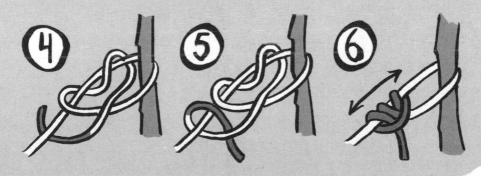

GO! WILD
STAFF PROFILE

ANNA CONDA

SERIOUSLY SCARY! TALKS IN SHORT BURSTS LIKE A MACHINE-GUN. OUTBACK SAID THAT ANNA KNOWS NINE DIFFERENT WAYS TO KILL SOMEONE WITH HER BARE HANDS. HE WASN'T JOKING!

ALWAYS WEARS DARK GLASSES. GERBIL RECKONS IF YOU LOOK HER IN THE EYES YOU TURN TO STONE!

MEGA MUSCLES

SERIOUS SCAR

EVEN MORE SERIOUS KNIFE!!

THESE BOOTS WERE MADE FOR STOMPING —ON PEOPLE, SAM SAYS.

14:30—THE FiRE PiT

For the afternoon session we were training at
THE FiRE PiT with the Wild Warriors. I saw them
whispering and laughing as we approached.

'They're starting to get on my nerves,' muttered Jas.

'Let's make sure we beat them at this then,'
I said. 'That'll shut them up!'

We gathered around a scorched metal table,
and Anna Conda showed us how to start a fire
with a ball of dry grass tinder, and a spark from a
FIRESTEEL. Again, it sounded easy enough, but
after my shelter-building disaster, I was starting to
worry that this whole bushcraft survival thing was
harder than it looked.

Each of us had to prepare and light a fire in order
to score maximum points for our squad. Anna told us
to shout FiRE! as soon as we had flames.

'Heard you got a bit wet this morning,' said Magpie
from across the table, smirking at me through the
plastic teeth of her stupid wolf hat.

I opened my mouth to reply, then discovered that my brain had forgotten to pack any witty comebacks for the trip. If I could get my fire going first, THAT would wipe the smug smile off her face.

I picked up the firesteel—two metal rods that you scraped together to make a spark hot enough to light a fire if you didn't have any matches. But what if one landed on my hand? Would it burn right through? Maybe that's how Survival Clive had lost his finger!

'D'you want me to get a grown-up to help you with that?' said Magpie, giving me a mean smile. 'That tracksuit looks pretty flammable. One stray spark and the whole lot could go up!'

I ignored her. She was winding me up. My tracksuit wouldn't really catch fire . . . would it?

I waited until Magpie wasn't looking, then rolled up my sleeves just in case.

The dry grass tinder ball I had to light sat on the table in front of me—all it needed was a spark.

Come on, Charlie! You can do this.

I took a deep breath,
and scraped the Firesteel—

SPARK!

It worked!
I was so surprised I almost dropped it.
Then I noticed that, despite the impressive shower
of sparks, my tinder hadn't actually ignited.

I tried again. This time my spark produced a thin curl of grey smoke twisting up from the nest of dry grass. The urge to punch the air and run around was hard to resist—but I wasn't there yet.

I remembered that Anna had blown into her tinder to encourage the flame. Carefully, I lifted the smouldering ball and blew. Nothing.

I tried again, and the smoke twitched like a cat's tail, but the grass still refused to ignite.

Across the table, Magpie had smoke too.

NO! I couldn't let her beat me!

I blew again, and the smoke flickered.

I blew harder, and for a second the insides of the ball glowed . . . but faded the moment I stopped.

Opposite, Magpie's tinder was pouring out smoke—she was going to win—again!

Come on fire—FLAME ON!

I filled my lungs with air and *BLEWWWWWWW!*

The tinder ball disintegrated like a firework, showering Magpie's wolf hat in glowing fragments. I stared in horror as the hot embers twisted the fake grey fur into a black smoking mess.

Magpie was so engrossed in her task, she hadn't noticed. I was starting to think I might get away with it, that the thing would just die out and she'd never know. Then my scattered tinder finally burst into life, sending flames licking across the wolf hat at frightening speed.

'FIRE!' shouted Magpie, as her own tinder ignited. 'I've got fire!'

You don't know the half of it, I thought.

Magpie pointed in triumph at the flickering fire on the bench in front of her, still oblivious to the one on top of her head. But other people had noticed. I had to do something.

When I grabbed for the hat Magpie tried to stop me, then she saw the flames and shrieked. I dropped the flaming wolf head onto the ground and stamped on it. But rather than going out, the fire spread—fizzing along the whiskers like a bomb fuse. Then I saw the fire bucket under the table . . .

Magpie stared at the remains of her hat smouldering under a pile of damp, dirty sand. For a second I thought she was going to cry, then she let out a roar, and lunged.

HOW TO BUILD A FIRE!

SURVIVAL TIP

If you find yourself stranded, and forced to make camp for the night, a toasty fire will not only provide warmth and heat for cooking, it will also lift your spirits and signal your position to the rescue party.

③ When the kindling is alight, add LARGER STICKS and logs. Dried animal droppings also burn well!

② Arrange KINDLING (dry twigs no thicker than your finger) in a teepee over the tinder.

① Use small, DRY, fibrous materials like bark shavings, dry grass and moss, cotton wool balls or tissue paper to make a TINDER BALL. Light with a match, or a spark from a FIRESTEEL.

REMEMBER: Be very careful near fire. Never leave a fire unattended.

20:14—THE STINK HOLE CONSPIRACY

Setting fire to Magpie's hat had been an ACCIDENT, but she had HIT ME on purpose! So it seemed totally unfair that we were given the same punishment, and had to empty the centre's chemical toilet together!

Outback handed us a large container of blue liquid and a pair of rubber gloves each.

'Piece of advice,' he said. 'Take a deep breath before you go in, then hold it for as long as you can. It's called the STINK HOLE for a reason!' Then he laughed and walked away to join the others who were playing football—yes, FOOTBALL!—on the grass outside the centre.

'This is your fault!' spat Magpie, as we walked across the yard. She had replaced the wolf hat with a woolly one. It made her look like an angry gnome.

'It was an accident!' I said. 'You didn't have to punch me! I can't believe Anna didn't give me any points either! I thought the object of the exercise was to start a fire!'

'Are you trying to be funny?' said Magpie. 'That's you all over isn't it? A JOKE. You AND your mates!'

'What? Just because we don't have stupid code names and dress up like we're in the army!' I snorted. 'I bet we finish higher than you at the end of the week.'

'Yeah?' Magpie stopped. 'I think I'll take that bet.'

'What?'

'You said that you BET your Misfits finish higher than the Wild Warriors. Or are you just all talk?'

An icy finger traced a line down my spine.

Technically that WAS what I'd said. Unfortunately, I hadn't actually meant I wanted to BET on it. But I couldn't back out now.

'OK—so what do we win?' I tried to sound like I made ridiculous bets with scary gnomes every day of my life.

'How much money have you got?' said Magpie.

'Not much.'

'A forfeit for the loser then,' she said.

'Like what?' I had a horrible vision of being forced to streak through the Go! Wild Mess Hall wearing nothing but a head-torch!

'The LEAP OF DOOM,' said Magpie.

I laughed. What was it with all the dramatic names in this place? The WALL OF THE WILD! That was just a tatty noticeboard with photos stuck to it. The STINK HOLE! OK, that one was probably fairly accurate judging by the smell wafting towards us—but the LEAP OF DOOM! Seriously?

'So what's that exactly?'

Magpie gave an evil grin. 'You'll see!'

I shrugged. 'OK.'

'And your whole squad has to do it,' said Magpie.

'No! This is just between me and you.'

She snorted. 'Why? Because your mates are too chicken!'

'No, they'd do anything your lot would do.'

'Good. So they can do it then. Whoever loses, the whole squad does THE LEAP.'

What choice did I have? Backing out would have meant admitting Magpie was right.

The others would understand . . . probably.

'Well?' said Magpie.

I nodded. 'OK.'

Magpie gave a scary smile and held out a rubber-gloved hand. 'You need to keep it quiet though,' she said. 'If Survival Clive finds out he'll say it's too dangerous and stop us!'

Our gloves squeaked as we shook, making me shiver, and I had the horrible feeling that I'd just made a huge mistake.

Then Magpie opened the door to the Stink Hole, and for the next ten minutes all I could think about was trying not to breathe!

3

FROM
BAD
TO
WORSE

07:14—GO! WILD MESS HALL

'You not eating that?' Sam's fork hovered over the sausage on my plate.

I shook my head.

'What's wrong with you?' he said, scraping the remains of my breakfast onto his own.

What was wrong with me? Answering THAT could be tricky. I tried out the conversation in my head:

Maybe now wasn't the best time to let the others know what I'd done—especially as I still wasn't sure exactly what I HAD DONE! Better to wait until I found out what the Leap of Doom was all about.

Of course, the best solution would be to make sure that the Misfits finished the week above the Wild Warriors on the Go! Wild leader board. That way the others would never need to know. We were only one point behind. How hard could it be?

09:07—FOOD GLORIOUS FOOD (GO! WILD TRAINING HALL)

'THE SURVIVAL RULE OF THREES,' said Survival Clive, holding up three fingers—except, in his case it was only two and a half! 'This rule states that we cannot last for more than three MINUTES without air; three DAYS without water; and three WEEKS without food.'

'Three weeks?' Jasmine whispered. 'Sam couldn't last three hours!'

I smiled, then turned back to my notebook. I needed to concentrate if we were going to beat the Wild Warriors today.

WHEN ON THE TRAIL IT'S VITAL TO KEEP WELL HYDRATED. THE COLOUR OF YOUR WEE IS A USEFUL WARNING SYSTEM!

SURVIVAL TIP

WEE GAUGE

LIGHT YELLOW
GOOD

DARK YELLOW
WATER
DRINK

ORANGE/RED
DOCTOR!

WEE GAUGE

For the next forty minutes Survival Clive gave a slideshow about edible plants we might find in the forest. I took notes and did some drawings, so I'd remember which wild berries would be safe to eat if our food supplies ran out.

'Building shelter and collecting firewood uses energy,' said Survival Clive, 'which means food IS important. But, in any survival situation, your FIRST PRIORITY is finding WATER. Without it you'll be dead in a few days.' He paused to let this fact sink in.

'If you're injured and it's hot, you'd be lucky to last that long. Even a fit person will find it harder to think and perform simple tasks after just a few hours without water. In a survival situation, making a bad decision could KILL YOU!

'One time in the Kenyan savannah,' said Clive, 'I was so desperate for fluid, I squeezed the liquid from fresh elephant dung and drank that.'

RATHER YOU THAN ME, MATE!

A collective EEWWWW rang out across the room.

'It wasn't the tastiest drink I've ever had,' said Survival Clive, grinning, 'but it saved my life—as did the ants and spiders I've eaten. Now—I'm not expecting you to resort to such things when you GO WILD tomorrow—for a start, there's a distinct shortage of elephant dung round here! However, we wouldn't want you to feel left out, so we've prepared a BUSH TUCKER lunch box for each of you now.'

'I'm not eating elephant poo!' said Gerbil.

Survival Clive smiled. 'Well, that's up to you, but don't forget there are points at stake.'

Not just points, I thought, glancing across at Magpie. She was wearing her wolf hat again. The blackened fur and melted whiskers made it look like the headdress of some demonic witch-doctor.

I knew I could rely on Sam if the task involved food, but I was worried about Jasmine and Gerbil. I was beginning to wish I'd told them about the BET and what was REALLY at stake if we lost. But there was no time for that now.

'What if it is elephant poo?' said Gerbil.

'It won't be,' I said. 'Survival Clive told us it's all safe to eat.'

Jasmine frowned. 'That doesn't mean it's going to taste nice,' she said, and lifted the lid on the first box.

19

'That looks like wee!' said Gerbil.

On the Warriors table, Magpie nudged Falcon. 'Go on, Fal—just drink it—she's too chicken.'

Falcon lifted the glass and gave the liquid a sniff. 'D'you think it IS wee?'

'Of course not!' said Owl. 'It looks like some kind of tea—nettle probably.'

Sam's eyes widened. 'As in STINGING nettles?'

'Yeah,' said Magpie. 'You gotta drink it fast or your tongue swells up and you can't breathe.'

Jasmine frowned. 'I'm not stupid, you know!' She snatched up the beaker and downed the yellow liquid in a single gulp.

'Go Jas!' I said.

EMPTY!

Then Falcon drank hers, so the scores were level.
'What was it?' said Gerbil.

'Nettle tea,' said Survival Clive, 'just as Owl
suspected. Full of vitamins, and said to be able to
cure anything from the common cold to diarrhoea!
And just for the record, it does not retain any of its
stinging properties once brewed!'

After Jasmine's challenge had turned out to
be relatively harmless, Gerbil was looking quite
relaxed—until he opened box number TWO.

'O. M. G!' said Jasmine.

JUICY!

HEAD!

LEGS!!

NUTRITIOUS!

'For our next course we have a delicious, nutritious, juicy, edible worm,' said Survival Clive.'

'A . . . WORM?' Gerbil's voice had gone wobbly.

I glanced across at the Wild Warriors and saw Hawk pick up her worm. She put it into her mouth, chewed, swallowed, and didn't even flinch. Magpie cheered.

I put my arm around Gerbil's shoulders. 'Come on Gerb, you can do it!'

'But . . . it's a worm,' said Gerbil.

'An EDIBLE one,' said Sam.

Gerbil looked at him. 'It's STILL a WORM!'

'Just close your eyes and pretend it's a Twiglet.'

'A TWIGLET? I hate Twiglets!'

72

'Well, what DO you like?' I said.

'I like chips.'

'Pretend it's a chip then!'

'Yeah, one of those crunchy brown ones at the bottom of the packet,' said Sam.

'You can do it Gerb,' I said quietly. 'We can't let that lot think we're scared.'

Gerbil took a deep breath, then he closed his eyes and reached into the box. But the moment his fingers touched the worm, he dropped it like he'd been bitten.

The Wild Warriors laughed.

'It's a chip,' I said. 'Focus on the chip.'

'All crunchy and covered in vinegar,' said Sam.

'Delicious,' said Jasmine.

Gerbil nodded and picked up the worm. 'It's a crunchy chip,' he said, eyes still closed. 'I like chips.'

His hand hovered in mid-air. I could see ridges on the worm's body, a row of pointy feet, and a head with eyes. I prayed that Gerbil would keep his closed.

Then he did it—

There was a CRUNCH—

'Don't stop!' said Sam. 'Chew fast and swallow!'

'Tasty chip,' I said.

Gerbil's face twisted as he chewed—it looked like his mouth was playing tug of war with the rest of his features. Finally, he swallowed.

'That did NOT taste like a chip!' he said.

I hugged him. 'Gerbil—you THE MAN!'

ROUND 3

SAM VS OWL

'OK,' said Survival Clive. 'Both squads have four points and no refusals.' He grinned. 'But let's see how you get on with box number three.'

'About time,' said Sam, rubbing his hands. 'I'm starving!' He lifted the lid.

DISH #3: FRIED CRICKET
AND GREEN LEAF SALAD

SAM WON'T EAT THE SALAD!

'WHAT—IS—THAT?' Jasmine covered her mouth.

'Fried cricket,' Survival Clive said. 'Full of protein.'

'My favourite!' Sam grabbed the cricket and tossed it into his mouth. He smiled at the Wild Warriors as he chewed, then licked his lips. 'DEE—LI—CIOUS!!! Got any more?'

Survival Clive laughed. 'Good man! Misfits take the lead. Over to you girls.'

Owl's face had gone pale. 'We didn't have to do this last year,' she said, in an unusually small voice, glancing at us, then back at the insect in the box.

Falcon and Magpie were looking worried. For a moment I was sure Owl was going to refuse, then Hawk hissed into her ear. Owl nodded and reached for the cricket. Her hand was shaking as she put it into her mouth, and there were tears in her eyes— but she kept chewing until the insect was gone.

'All level!' said Survival Clive. 'This one's going right to the wire.'

Which is when I remembered . . .

It was MY turn next.

I'd been worried about Jas and Gerbil, but it was me who let everyone down! My failure to eat the scorpion left us three points behind the Wild Warriors, with one training session to go—our last chance to catch up before the forest trial itself.

We were learning how to use a compass and read a map. At least, that was the idea. Unfortunately, my compass seemed to have a mind of its own, and the map made as much sense to me as a dot-to-dot picture with the numbers removed!

Sam and Gerbil weren't much better, but Jasmine seemed to get the hang of it. When Survival Clive told us to head on a particular bearing, Jas would nod, twist the compass, and point. The rest of us simply followed her.

Using this method we managed to collect another six squad points, which put us just one behind the Wild Warriors, and up to third on the leader board!

FINDING YOUR WAY
WITHOUT A COMPASS

If you find yourself lost without a compass, use a STICK and the SUN to get your bearings.

SUN

SURVIVAL TIP

① Push a STICK into the ground.

③ Wait 15 minutes then mark the end of the new shadow.

SOUTH

② Mark end of shadow.

EAST

90° angle

WEST

NORTH ④ Draw a line between the two points to find EAST and WEST.

A line at 90° to the first, gives you NORTH and SOUTH.

It had occurred to me that Outback might know something about the Leap of Doom, so when I saw him in the yard after dinner, hosing down one of the Go! Wild Land Rovers, I sneaked out to ask him.

'Not thinking of trying it are you?' He switched off the hose and grinned.

I tried to sound disinterested. 'Nah, I just heard someone talking, and wondered what it was.'

Outback nodded, but I'm not sure he believed me. 'It's pretty radical!' he said. 'I've got a video of the last kid who tried it! Should be here somewhere...' He pulled a mobile from his shorts and thumbed the screen. 'Fool did it for a bet! How dumb is that!' Outback laughed and handed me the phone.

The picture was fuzzy, but what I could see was enough to turn my stomach to a watery mush.

'It's just over that ridge in the forest,' said Outback. 'Place called DEVIL FALLS. There's a waterfall with a deep pool below. Gotta be a good twenty-metre dive!'

In the video, the tiny figure on the cliff top hesitated, rocking backwards and forwards on his heels. I tried to imagine what must have been going through his mind—that this could be the last thing he EVER did.

LONG WAY DOWN ↓

Then he went.
A short run up and a LEAP over the edge...

frozen
for a
moment
in
mid-air
...

then

down,

arms

and legs

flailing

until...

SPLASH!

The image shook and the sound distorted as the people watching clapped and cheered, but you could hear the anxiety in their voices, until the figure finally surfaced and waved.

I returned the phone to Outback, hoping he wouldn't notice how much my hand was shaking.

'Pretty wild, huh!' He grinned. 'Now you see why they call it the Leap of Doom? You gotta be crazy to try a stunt like that!'

I nodded.

WHAT HAD I DONE?

We were still one point behind the Wild Warriors. Unless we beat them in the forest, it would be me, Sam, Jas, and Gerbil up there on Devil Falls!

Last year the Wild Warriors had won! What chance did WE have? What had I been THINKING to make a bet like that?

But that has always been my problem—
I DON'T THINK!

I was thinking now all right though. Thinking about what Sam was going to say when he found out.

Sam hated HEIGHTS. In fact, the only thing that Sam hated more than heights, was WATER!

He was going to kill me.

Then I thought about Jas. She'd bring me back to life, just so she could kill me again herself!

Even Gerbil was going to struggle to keep smiling through this one.

And if I survived telling my friends what I'd done, the Leap of Doom would finish me off.

4

GOING WILD!

10:04—EXPEDITION BRIEFING

By the time we gathered in the barn for Survival
Clive's expedition briefing next morning, I had
decided there was nothing to be gained by telling
the others about the Leap of Doom. In fact, it was
fairly clear to me that my well-being depended
upon them NOT finding out. Which left me with one
option: I had to make sure that we beat the Wild
Warriors in the Forest Survival Challenge.

   'At thirteen hundred hours,' said Survival Clive,
'each squad will be driven to a different location
inside the two hundred and fifty square miles of
forest. You will have nothing but the equipment
you carry and the skills you have learnt, to help you
survive for four days and three nights in the wild.
You will need to build shelter, collect water, make a
fire to cook and keep warm.'

   He paused and pointed at us. 'But remember—
sometimes it is the person with the strongest will,
not the greatest skill, who survives.'

If that was true, maybe I had a chance after all!

Survival Clive pressed a button, and a map appeared on the screen behind him. It was covered in a rash of tiny green flags.

'Your objective is to collect as many of these checkpoint flags as you can, and then navigate back here. Each flag is worth two points. The first squad home gets an extra four points, the second— three, and so on. You may be interested to know that these checkpoints will also contain supplies—food, equipment, water—so you'll want to make sure that your squad gets there first!'

'Sounds like The Hunger Games!' muttered Jasmine.

'Except we don't have to kill the other players,' said Gerbil, then he frowned. 'We don't, do we?'

Expecting a week at a football training camp, none of us had packed much except our kit and boots. So, while we were at the briefing, Doug took the Frankenbus into the town to find some outdoor clothing and equipment. It wasn't a successful trip. Half the stuff was the wrong size, and the rest looked like he'd raided a circus clown costume shop! I decided to stick with my tracksuit and trainers (and hope it didn't rain!), but there was no alternative to the ADVENTURE KITTEN rucksack with matching sleeping bag and water bottle.

The Wild Warriors laughed so hard when they saw us, it made their camouflage face paint run.

BRIGHT ORANGE RUCKSACK

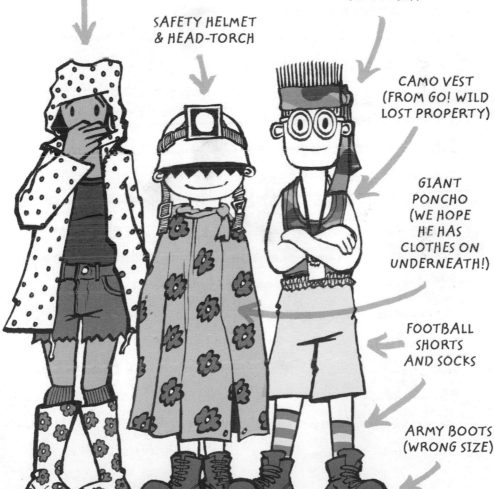

13:51—THE DROP-OFF
(CRAWDALE FOREST, LOCATION UNKNOWN)

It felt like we'd been driving for miles when the Frankenbus finally stopped.

'Right,' said Outback, as we climbed out. 'Last chance to check your gear. Once Doug drives away it's just us and the bush for the next four days!'

Each squad was taking an OBSERVER into the forest with them. This person wouldn't be allowed to help complete the mission. They were purely there to make sure we didn't do anything stupid—like dying! Outback had been assigned to come with us.

'I'll just do a radio check then we're good to go,' he said, pulling out a walkie-talkie. 'Wild Camp Three Zero, this is Wild Bush Mobile Five Nine, over—'

The handset spat static, then Survival Clive's voice crackled through the air. 'Wild Bush Mobile Five Nine this is Wild Camp Three Zero, reading you loud and clear.'

'Well, I'll be off then,' said Doug. 'Good luck!'

'What are you going to do while we're gone?' Jasmine asked him.

'Now we're out of the way,' said Outback. 'Survival Clive will unlock the Secret Room—the one with the widescreen TV and games console!' He laughed, but I wasn't sure that he was joking.

We waved as the Frankenbus gave a final exhaust-gun-salute and drove away. When the smoke cleared, I saw we were on a long straight track with dense trees on either side. I pictured all the flags hidden away in there waiting to be found.

'OK, so let's go!' I said.

'Before you go rushing off,' said Jasmine. 'It might help to work out where we are first. So we know what direction to GO in.'

She unfolded her map and we gathered round.

It was impossible to walk in a straight line through the forest, and the further we went, the thicker the undergrowth became.

Every so often Jas stopped to check the map.

'We're a bit off course,' she said, for the third time. 'We need to head more that way.'

'Do you know where we are yet?' I asked.

'Down here I think—but we could do with a landmark to get a bearing. Who wants to climb a tree and have a look around?'

Sam paled—we all knew he was scared of heights.

'I'd do it, but I have this problem with gravity,' said Gerbil. 'It means I'm a lot better at falling out of trees than climbing up them.'

'Yeah,' I said. 'I think I have that too!'

Jasmine stared at us. 'You mean none of you can climb a tree?' She sighed and handed me the map. 'Hold this.'

Leaves floated down as Jasmine disappeared into the branches. A moment later a disembodied voice called down. 'Wow! This forest is huge!'

'What can you see?' I shouted.

'Lots of trees!'

'Great,' I said. 'We can see those from down here!'

'Hang on!' The tree shook as Jasmine moved around, sending more leaves and a few branches crashing down. 'Sorry!'

Moments later she was back on the ground.

'I think I saw the river,' she said, taking the map back from me and pulling out her compass. 'So that means we must be . . . here!' Beside Jasmine's finger on the map was a little green flag.

'We're right next to A FLAG!' I said.

'Not exactly NEXT TO!' said Jas. 'This is a SCALE map, Charlie. Four centimetres on here is one kilometre in real life!'

'So how far is that flag?'

'About . . . half a kilometre . . . that way.' She pointed.

'YES!' I said. 'Let's GO!'

NAISMITH'S RULE

TELLS YOU HOW LONG IT WILL TAKE TO REACH YOUR DESTINATION.

5KM 3MILES = ONE HOUR WALKING

—ADD THIRTY MINUTES FOR EVERY 300M UPHILL
—TAKE AWAY TEN MINUTES FOR EVERY 300M DOWNHILL
(FOR STEEP DOWNHILL SLOPES, ADD TEN MINUTES!)

'Shouldn't we be there by now?' I unhooked a bramble from my tracksuit and winced as the needle thorns drew blood.

'It can't be much further,' said Jasmine.

'I wish they'd get a move on.'

Outback, Sam, and Gerbil were strolling along

behind us like they were out on a Sunday picnic. It hadn't occurred to me that they wouldn't want to bother looking for flags. I blamed Outback—his laid-back Surfer Dude routine was rubbing off on my friends.

'You really want to find that flag don't you?' said Jasmine.

'I thought that was the whole point.'

Jas laughed. 'I just came for the holiday. I'd be quite happy to find a nice sunny spot to camp for a few days. All this tramping through the undergrowth seems a lot of effort just to collect some stupid flags.'

'But we need the points, or we'll end up LAST!'

'So what?' said Jasmine. 'Does it really matter if we DO come last?'

And there it was—the perfect opportunity to tell Jasmine about the bet. I could ask her to help me motivate the others into action. Except that wasn't what would happen. If Jas found out, she'd be more likely to throw me over the Leap of Doom herself!

An hour later, we still hadn't found the flag.

'I vote we set up camp,' said Sam. 'These boots are killing my feet, and if I don't eat something soon I'm gonna collapse. Remember, Survival Clive said that hunger can affect your judgement.'

Sam started walking, then suddenly veered off and crashed into a tree.

'See!' he said, getting to his feet. 'It's going already!'

Outback laughed.

'Come on Sam!' I said. 'We haven't got time to mess about! WE NEED TO FIND THE FLAG!'

I realized I was shouting.

'Charlie!' said Outback. 'You gotta learn to chillax, man!'

'I think we're lost anyway,' said Jas. 'I could do with some time to look at the map again.'

We found a suitable spot and set to work rigging a series of tarpaulin shelters. I remembered my last disastrous attempt and my heart sank. Then I saw

Sam dragging half a tree across the clearing and had an idea—if I made a wood shelter I wouldn't need to tie any knots!

Survival Clive had told us that the ability to adapt was essential in a survival situation. Maybe I wasn't so bad at this after all.

Searching for building materials helped take my mind off the fact that we'd been in the forest for a whole afternoon and failed to find a single flag. I didn't want to think about how many the Wild Warriors might have collected already. Instead, I concentrated on constructing my sleeping quarters for the night ahead.

My finished berth looked a lot like the skeleton of an ancient wooden dinosaur, with more gaps than was probably ideal, but on the whole I was pleased.

'Wow!' said Gerbil.

I turned around, trying not to make my grin too obvious, then realized that Gerbil wasn't looking at my shelter.

'Sam! That's incredible!' said Jasmine.

'Yeah! Can I sleep over at yours tonight?'
said Gerbil.

Then Outback emerged from his tent—that's
right—a TENT! So much for "I like to make a proper
shelter from what nature provides!"

'Nice crib,' he said, holding out his fist for Sam. 'Respect, dude!'

Outback glanced around the camp—taking in Gerbil's hammock and tarp combo, Jasmine's shelter with its thick bed of ferns. Finally he came to mine.

'You've even got a fire built ready,' he said.

'No! That's my . . .' I began, then realized they were all laughing.

'It's not finished yet!' I stammered, feeling my cheeks go red.

'Don't worry, Charlie, I've seen worse!' Outback grinned and put an arm round my shoulders. 'I'd go easy on the beans tonight though, mate. Let one off in there, and you'll blow the whole lot down!'

21:25—NIGHT CAMP

'Wild Camp Three Zero,
this is Wild Bush Mobile Five Nine, over—'
Outback was doing the evening radio check to
let Survival Clive know we were still alive. He also
had to report any flags found so the maps and leader
board could be updated. I could barely hear for the
blood thundering in my ears as I waited to find out
how far behind the Wild Warriors we were. When
the news came in that they hadn't found any flags
either, I leapt to my feet and punched the air.

'Charlie!' said Sam. 'Chillax man!'

Outback laughed. 'Don't take this the wrong way, mate, but you're not gonna win. If you want my advice . . .'

(Which I didn't—but he gave it anyway.)

'I'd forget about the flags and just enjoy some quality time hanging out in the wild.' He smiled. 'I say tomorrow we find a nice spot by the river and soak up some rays . . .'

'Or play some football,' said Sam.

Outback grinned. 'Play some football—why not— good call brother!'

Sam beamed and leaned back against his pack, in exactly the same pose as Outback.

'Sounds good to me,' said Jasmine.

I sighed. Maybe Magpie was right—we didn't belong here. But it was too late to back out now. We HAD to beat the Wild Warriors, which meant I needed the old Misfits back. The gang who would have been right there with me, wanting to wipe the smug smile off Magpie's face.

I was going to have to tell them about the bet.

But deciding to tell them, and actually finding the words, were two completely different things.

I looked out into the darkness of the forest, hoping for inspiration . . . and for a second, I saw two slits of yellow light among the trees.

'Did you see that?'

'What?' said Gerbil.

'There's something out there! I saw its eyes.'

Jas laughed. 'It's just your imagination, Charlie!'

'Not scared of the dark are you, mate?' said Sam, nudging Outback.

I waited for Outback to join in with some joke, but he didn't.

'Charlie could be right,' he said, his face serious. 'Some folk believe there's a wild beast living in this forest.'

'A BEAST?' Jasmine's eyes widened.

Outback nodded. 'Did you ever wonder how Survival Clive lost that finger and his eye?'

'The Beast took them?' said Gerbil.

'About three years ago,' Outback said, 'Survival Clive went out on his own to set up the flags for a Go! Wild challenge . . . and didn't come back. They found him two days later, barely alive, raving about some Beast—taller than a bear, with claws like the Wolverine!'

'That happened HERE? In this forest?' Gerbil looked around nervously.

Outback nodded.

'Has anyone seen it since?' said Sam.

'Every now and again someone comes back and says they HEARD something, or SAW something. Tracks too, and trees with giant claw marks scratched into the bark—but nobody's come face to face with it since Survival Clive . . . until now.'

They all looked at me.

Outback's teeth gleamed in the firelight. 'What do you reckon, Charlie? Did you just eyeball the Beast?'

I swallowed. 'I don't know. But there was definitely something.'

'You've got a walkie-talkie,' said Jasmine. 'Shouldn't you call it in?'

'And say what? That Charlie THINKS he saw something?' Outback shook his head. 'We get fined for making false distress calls.' He leaned forward and poked at the fire with a long stick. 'Might be an idea to set a watch though—keep the fire going through the night. That SHOULD keep it away . . .'

He pulled out the stick, sending a shower of orange sparks into the air. 'We could sharpen this and lash it to a long branch to make a spear, then whoever is on guard can protect themselves.'

Sam nodded grimly and started looking through the wood pile for a suitable branch.

'How big was it, Charlie?' said Gerbil.

'I don't know—I just saw its eyes.'

'I've heard it's taller than a man—maybe ten foot!' said Outback.

'TEN FOOT!' Gerbil's knees were shaking now.

'Hang on,' said Jasmine. 'If this thing is ten feet tall, its eyes would have been way up there.' She pointed up into the canopy. 'Charlie saw something down there.'

Outback shrugged. 'In that case you've got nothing to worry about. It was probably just a squirrel or something.'

'A squirrel?' Sam sounded disappointed.

'Squirrels are nice,' said Gerbil. 'They don't gouge people's eyes out.'

'Usually,' said Outback. 'Unless it's the Mutant Sabre-Toothed Squirrel Beast!' He grinned and started to laugh.

'Wait a minute!' Jasmine frowned. 'You're making this up!'

'What?' said Sam, who had just finished constructing the spear.

'So there is no Beast?' said Gerbil.

Jasmine shook her head. 'I don't know if I'm more angry, or relieved.'

'GAH!' said Sam, and hurled his spear into the ground.

23:36—LAST WORDS

I couldn't sleep. My Adventure Kitten sleeping bag offered about as much protection as a paper hat in a hail storm. The wind had also changed direction and was blowing ashes from the fire directly into my poorly constructed wooden cage. Then there was the fact that Outback's Leap of Doom video seemed to be stuck on a loop in my head. But most of all, I was spooked.

Ten-Foot Mutant Sabre-Toothed Squirrel Beast or not, I'd seen SOMETHING—and I was fairly sure it was still out there. I could feel it watching us from the darkness, waiting for me to fall asleep so it could sneak into the camp—past the fire we had allowed to go out and Sam's spear discarded on the ground—and eat us.

When we failed to call in tomorrow morning, Survival Clive would try to contact Outback on his walkie-talkie . . .

But when the search party eventually discovered our camp, there would be nothing left but piles of bones—

and the final blood-splattered entry in this logbook.

Which means that these could be my last words . . .

GETTING WILDER

5

07:32—SNAKED

Sam's scream woke us up. It took me and Jas a few minutes to convince him that the ants had gone.

'Why did they bite me?' said Sam.

'They probably didn't appreciate you sleeping on top of their nest,' said Jasmine.

I laughed. 'Especially after all the beans you ate last night!'

'It's not funny. I'm all itchy.' Sam shuddered. 'Are you sure they've all gone?'

'They were more interested in that packet of biscuits than you,' said Jas, pointing to where Sam's kit lay scattered on the ground. 'It's no wonder you've got ants—leaving all your stuff lying around like that.'

'I didn't!' Sam frowned. 'That was all in my bag when I went to sleep.'

'Has anyone seen my boots?' said Gerbil, peering out from under his tarp. 'I hung them on that branch last night.'

'Who cares about your boots!' said Sam. 'SOMEONE'S TAKEN MY FOOD!'

We heard the sound of a zip, and Outback's head emerged from his tent. 'Hey! What's with the racket, guys?'

'Someone's taken Sam's food and Gerbil's boots,' I said.

'You think it was the Mutant Sabre-Toothed Squirrel Beast?' said Gerbil, glancing round.

'What would a squirrel want with your boots?' said Jasmine.

Gerbil shrugged. 'He's a mutant. He might have man-feet!'

'This is SERIOUS!' said Sam. 'All I've got left is

half a packet of biscuits, and there's ants in them!'

Outback crawled from his tent and stood up. 'Sounds like you've been snaked,' he said.

'SNAKED?'

'It's what we call it when you raid someone else's camp,' said Outback. 'It happens a lot. Some squads will do anything to win.'

'Stealing people's stuff in the middle of the night!' said Jasmine. 'That's out of order!'

Outback shrugged. 'You snooze, you lose!'

'I bet it was the Wild Warriors,' said Gerbil.

Sam bent down and picked up the spear. 'Whoever it was, they made a big mistake when they took my food.' He growled. 'Come on, let's go after them. I want my breakfast back!'

I had to turn away so the others wouldn't see me grinning. I couldn't believe my luck—by raiding our camp, the Wild Warriors had accidentally motivated my squad into action!

'Um, slight problem,' said Gerbil. 'I haven't got any boots.'

'I've got these.' Jasmine pulled a pair of flowery flip-flops from her rucksack.

I was about to laugh, when Sam grabbed them.

'Gerb can have my boots,' he said, sitting down and tugging at the laces. 'They're killing my feet. I'd rather wear these.'

We stared at him.

'What?' said Sam. 'Have you never seen a bloke in flip-flops before?'

11:46—WHAT HAVE YOU DONE WITH THE REAL CHARLIE MERRICK?

We'd been marching for hours with no sign of the Wild Warriors. Sam was getting angrier with every step, slashing at the undergrowth with his spear and muttering murderous promises about what he was going to do when we caught up with them.

'How about a song?' said Gerbil.

> 'I DON'T KNOW BUT I'VE BEEN TOLD,
> WARRIORS STINK LIKE FOOT-CHEESE MOULD.'

Outback laughed and joined in—

> 'I DON'T KNOW BUT IT'S BEEN SAID,
> THEY RAID YOUR CAMP WHEN YOU'RE IN BED.'

Then together—

> 'SAM'S GETTING HUNGRY.
> AIN'T GONNA BE FUNNY.
> WILD WARRIORS—YOU'RE DEAD!'

'Too right,' growled Sam, grinning.

We made up extra verses, each one more vicious and bloodthirsty than the last. It wasn't the best song in the world, but it kept us going, and helped Sam forget how hungry he was—for a while at least!

SINGING WHILE ON A LONG MARCH CAN RAISE THE SPIRITS AND KEEP EVERYONE GOING.

SURVIVAL TIP

We were halfway through a verse that rhymed ANTS with PANTS, when we stepped out into a wide area of lush green grass. After so long picking our way through trees and tangled undergrowth, it felt like paradise.

'Wow! What is THAT?' said Gerbil, pointing to a tall wooden structure at the far side of the field.

'Must be part of the Sculpture Trail,' said Jasmine. 'There was a leaflet back at the centre.'

'Looks like goalposts to me!' said Sam. 'Get the ball out, Charlie!'

'We haven't got time to play football!' I said, thinking about all the flags we still needed to find.

'No time for football!' Jasmine stared at me. 'OK. Where's the real Charlie Merrick? What have you done with him?' She walked over and peered down the back of my collar.

'What are you doing?'

'Looking for the OFF switch, you evil alien robot replica!'

I shrugged her away. 'Seriously, we need to keep moving!'

ROBOT REPLICA ME!

'I'm hungry,' said Sam. 'I need food—then football—THEN I'll be ready to catch me some Wild Warriors!' He threw the spear and it landed quivering in the ground.

'I think we should feed him,' said Jas. 'It might be safer for everyone.'

With Sam's rations gone, we divided up what was left between the four of us. The way Sam ate, it wasn't going to last the rest of the week. We had another problem too.

'Has anyone got any water left?' said Gerbil. 'I'm out.'

'Same here,' said Sam.

When Survival Clive had talked about running out of water back at the camp, it had seemed over-dramatic. Now it looked inevitable.

'Once Sam's finished spearing Wild Warriors, we'd better find that river,' said Jasmine.

WATER
TRAP & SOCK FILTER

WARNING—Apart from rain water you collect yourself, all other water found in a survival situation MUST be treated before it is safe to drink.

① Rain water is the safest source of water to drink. Use a CLEAN TARPAULIN, PONCHO, PLASTIC BAG etc. The larger the surface, the more water you will collect. Hang the tarp so that the water runs off into a CLEAN container.

② FILTER water to remove visible dirt particles before purifying. Improvise a filter using a CLEAN SOCK or water bottle. Fill the sock with layers of pebbles, gravel, sand and charcoal.

WEIGHT (stone) to direct flow

DIRTY WATER IN.

(Chunkiest at top.)

PEBBLES

COARSE GRAVEL

FINE GRAVEL

CHARCOAL

FINE SAND (tiny grains at bottom.)

CLEAN WATER OUT.

③ Once your water has been filtered, BOIL it for FIVE minutes and it will be safe to drink once cool. Store in clean, sealed containers.

I was repacking my rucksack when
Outback spotted the football.

'So you lot are a team,'
he said. 'You any good?'

WE DID—
BUT THAT'S
ANOTHER
STORY!

'We played at the World Cup!' said Sam.

'Yeah! And my aunt's a ridge-backed orang-utan!'

'I can see the family resemblance,' said Jasmine.

Outback laughed. 'Come on then, let's have a
game. Show me how good you are.'

'We haven't got time,' I said. 'We need to catch
up with the Wild Warriors and find some water!'

'Ha!' said Outback. 'Excuses! Bet you're rubbish!'

'Come on, Charlie!' Sam gave me puppy eyes—
which was both disturbing AND impossible to resist.

'OK,' I said. 'First to five, then we need to go.'

'Me and Jasmine, versus you three,' said Outback.
'I reckon we can take 'em, Jas—what d'you think?'

Jasmine sighed and took off her sunglasses.
'If I must!'

'Don't forget I'm wearing flip-flops,' said Sam.
'So you've got an advantage.'

'Yeah, and I'm wearing wellies,' said Jasmine. 'Shut up and play!'

'Four-one!' said Outback, reeling round arms aloft.
   He was annoyingly good, and Jasmine's initial reluctance had been replaced by a bloodthirsty enthusiasm for crunching tackles and pile-driver shots. She'd almost knocked Sam unconscious when he'd been foolish enough to get in the way of one.

Another goal and they'd win. It was no fun and we were wasting time. So when Sam threw the ball out, I ACCIDENTALLY let it slip through to Outback. Had he just run towards goal, Outback would probably have scored and won the game, but he couldn't resist an opportunity to show off. When his TRIPLE-STEP-OVER-REVERSE-FLICK-WITH-PIROUETTE sent him face first into the grass, Gerbil pounced on the loose ball and booted it to me.

Eager to avoid another shin-busting tackle from Jas, I hit a first-time shot and groaned as it sailed miles over the 'goal', disappearing into the forest with a sound of tearing branches.

'You can get that,' said Outback.

After the open sunlit clearing it seemed very dark among the trees, and I couldn't see the ball anywhere.

I heard the snap of twigs behind me and jumped.

Gerbil grinned. 'Just us,' he said, as Jasmine appeared next to him.

'Did you think it was the Mutant Sabre-Toothed Squirrel Beast?'

'Ha ha!' I said, stamping through the undergrowth.

'A lost ball means it's a draw by the way,' said Gerbil, giving me a wink.

'Is that so?' said Jasmine. 'Good job I found it then.' She reached into a clump of waist-high grass and held up the ball.

'Worth a try, Gerb,' I said, then froze. 'LOOK!' I pointed into the trees, just beyond where Jasmine stood with the football in her hands.

'A FLAG!' said Gerbil.

The flag was bright green. On the ground next to it was a large plastic barrel filled with water.

'Two in one!' I said. 'Result!'

Gerbil caught my arm. 'It's too easy.' He frowned. 'It could be a trap!'

'What d'you mean?'

'You touch that and a big boulder will come rolling out of the trees like in Indiana Jones!' he said.

'Really?' Jasmine sighed. 'Meanwhile back on Planet Earth . . .'

She plucked the flag from the ground and shook her head.

We walked back into the sunlight and I waved our trophy in the air.

'Look what we found!' I shouted.

I thought Sam would be pleased, but he and Outback were arguing.

'What's up?'

'I SAW something,' said Sam, his face pale, 'but he won't believe me!'

'What? Like the Mutant Sabre-Toothed Squirrel Beast?' said Gerbil, glancing round.

'I don't know WHAT it was,' said Sam. 'I just saw something big and black, over there in the trees.'

'You sure it wasn't a dog?' said Jasmine.

'With TUSKS?'

'Tusks!' Gerbil swallowed. 'Like sabre-toothed tusks?'

Outback was laughing. 'Nice try, Sam,' he said. 'But you can't use the same joke back on me. It won't work.'

'I'm NOT joking,' said Sam.

I've known Sam for most of my life—I can tell when he's being serious . . . AND when he's scared.

A sudden wind whipped across the field making the trees hiss, then the sun ducked behind a cloud, and a cold shadow crept over the grass.

'Time to move,' said Outback. 'Looks like rain.'

There's rain, and then there's—STANDING IN THE SHOWER WITH YOUR CLOTHES ON—RAIN! I could feel it running down my back and squelching inside my trainers.

But we had a flag—and some water, though I was starting to think I might have overdone it on the rehydration. I called a halt for a toilet break.

'You're having a laugh, Charlie!' said Outback. 'I'm not standing round in THIS, waiting while you water the weeds. You'll have to catch us up.'

I watched them walk away, listening until the sound of their voices faded and all I could hear was the rattle of rain on the leaves.

Suddenly I had the feeling I was being watched again, and remembered the look on Sam's face. What HAD he seen? It probably WAS just a dog or something. Even with his glasses on Sam's eyesight wasn't the best.

I leaned the flag against a tree while I did what I needed, and tried to ignore the rash of goosebumps spreading along my arms. The quicker I caught up with the others, the better.

But when I turned around I couldn't remember which way they'd gone.

All the trees looked the same!

I felt a flash of panic. What if I couldn't find them? It would be dark in a few hours. I'd be stranded on my own!

A branch crashed somewhere nearby, and my heart almost leapt out of my mouth. I spun round, but of course there was nothing there.

Come on Charlie, get a grip!

I started walking in the direction I thought the others had gone, then realized I was no longer carrying the flag. I'D LEFT IT BY THE TREE!

Cursing my stupidity, I turned back—

Which is when I discovered that something HAD been watching me after all.

Because there it was in front of me—

All yellow eyes, matted black fur and teeth . . .

I screamed.

I'd like to tell you that it was more a shriek of surprise than your actual—I THINK I JUST WET MYSELF BECAUSE I'M SO SCARED—kind of scream. But I'd be lying.

It took a few seconds for my petrified brain to register that beneath the twisted whiskers and yellowing teeth, there was a human face—smeared with camouflage paint—laughing at me.

'What was THAT?' said Magpie. 'Was that you? Or is there a six-year-old girl hiding behind that tree?'

I was about to reply when I noticed Magpie was holding a flag. 'Hey! That's OUR flag.'

'Not any more,' she said.

'Give it back!'

'You want it. Come and get it.' Magpie moved into a fighting stance, holding the flag like a staff.

'Charlie?' It was Jasmine's voice, distant in the trees. 'Where are you?'

'Over here!' I called, then turned back to Magpie. 'Now you're in tro—

But Magpie had vanished—along with the flag.

133

18:57—COLD BEANS & EVIL SCHEMES

'I can't believe you just let them take it!' said Sam, for the fifth time.

The others had assumed I'd been ambushed by the entire Warriors squad, and I hadn't quite got around to correcting them.

We were huddled together under a tarpaulin eating cold beans straight from the tin, while Outback radioed base and got an update on the leader board.

Survival Clive's voice faded in and out of the static, but we heard enough. The Wild Warriors had reported six flags found, and were leading by a massive eight points.

I buried my head in my hands. It was over. I was doomed—literally!

'How can they have found SIX?' said Jas, updating the map. 'Some of those flags are miles apart.'

'Maybe they're ambushing the other squads too,' said Gerbil. 'Taking the flags off them.'

I lifted my head.

'That's it!' I said. 'Gerbil—you're a genius!'

'I am?' He grinned. 'Erm . . . why?'

'That's how we can beat them! We snake the Wild Warriors and take THEIR flags!'

'Now you're talking!' said Sam.

'But don't we need to find them first?' said Gerbil, and my body sagged.

He was right. So far our attempts to catch up with the Wild Warriors had been a complete failure.

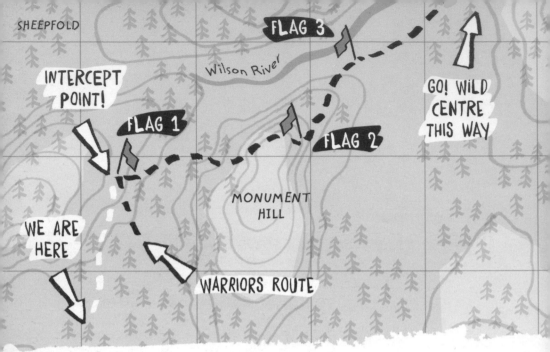

'Yeah, but now we know where they're going . . .' said Jasmine.

'We do?'

She pointed to the map. 'They'll be working their way back towards the Go! Wild Centre. There are three flags between here and there. Even if they are stealing off other squads, they won't miss the chance to pick up a couple of extras on the way.'

'So if we get there first,' I said.

'Payback time!' growled Sam.

ANOTHER
ONE OF
THOSE WEIRD
SCULPTURES!

08:42—ON A MISSION!

The gang was back! Next morning, we couldn't wait
to get going. When Gerbil announced that we'd
almost run out of food, Sam grinned.

'Don't worry, we'll get some off the Wild Warriors!'
'There'll be supplies at the flags too,' said Jasmine.

The sun was shining as we set off through the
steaming forest, wading through patches of mist
lingering in the hollows like swamp gas. We passed
more of the sculptures on the trail . . .

An hour and a half later we reached the first flag—
or rather, the hole in the ground where it had been.

'The Wild Warriors must be ahead of us,' said Jas.

Sam growled and kicked at the empty supplies box.
'I bet that had food in it!'

'So let's get going to the next one!' I said.

'Hang on!' Jas unfolded the map. 'We don't know
how far ahead they are, but chances are we won't
catch them.'

She was right. The vision of us standing at the top
of Devil Falls flickered into
full technicolour again.

'Unless,' said Jasmine.
(Unless was good!)

'We forget about the
second flag—' said Jas,
'and go straight for the
last one by the river.'

I looked at the map.
'If we cut across country
we could beat them to it!'

17:46—THE RIVER

We'd been fighting our way through densely packed trees and knotty undergrowth for hours. I was glad I had long trousers—Sam's legs were bleeding from all the brambles he'd waded through, but he wasn't the only one complaining. Gerbil had fallen into a patch of stinging nettles, and Jas was being eaten alive by bugs.

'This is ridiculous,' said Jasmine. 'I don't know why I let you talk me into it!'

'Me?'

'Yes, YOU!' They chorused.

I was about to remind them how good they would feel when we took our revenge on the Wild Warriors, when I heard something. 'Listen!'

'What?' Gerbil looked worried.

'Water!' said Jasmine.

We raced towards the sound and emerged from the trees at the top of a steep bank. I could see the river sparkling down below.

'This is it!' I said. 'The flag should be just down there.'

'Finally!' said Sam, and launched himself down the slope like a skier—except Sam was wearing flip-flops, not skis—and there was no snow. He slid most of the way on his backside and landed with a crash of snapping twigs, sending up a shower of leaves. For a second there was silence, then we heard a muffled voice float up from below. 'I'm OK!'

When we got to the bottom, Sam was waiting.

'I found the flag,' he said. 'But there's a great big river in the way!'

'What?' I could see the object of our quest fluttering in the trees on the opposite bank. 'But it's supposed to be on THIS SIDE!'

'Or maybe WE'RE supposed to be on THAT side,' said Gerbil.

It was a disaster! Any moment now the Wild Warriors would turn up and claim the flag right under our noses. Then they would disappear into the forest and we'd lose our one chance to track them.

'We've got to find a way across,' I said.

'Well, unless you can fly, you're out of luck,' said Jasmine, handing me the map. 'There's nowhere to cross for miles.'

'I could swim.'

'Have you seen how fast the current's going? You'd be swept away in seconds.'

I stared at her.

'There HAS to be a way!'

Gerbil put a hand on my shoulder. 'Sorry Charlie, but I don't think we're going to win this one.'

143

'But you don't understand!' I said, my voice getting louder. 'WE HAVE TO!'

'What d'you mean, we HAVE to?' Jas folded her arms.

'It's just a stupid survival competition,' said Sam.

I looked at them.

'What's going on, Charlie?' Jasmine's eyes narrowed.

I glanced at the river, glistening in the early evening sunshine, then looked back at my friends and took a deep breath.

'Now, don't go mad, but there's something I need to tell you . . .'

Sam only watched half the Leap of Doom video before returning the mobile to Outback.

'WHY would you make a bet like THAT?' he said, his face a mixture of fear and fury.

'I didn't want Magpie to think we were chicken!'

'Who cares what SHE thinks?' said Jasmine.

'Why didn't you tell us?' said Gerbil.

'I didn't want you to worry.'

'Worry?' Sam gave a bitter laugh. 'Why would we worry? Oh, yes—because you told Magpie we'd jump off a cliff if they beat us! Thanks, Charlie! You're a real mate!'

'I'm sorry! But I did it for YOU! The Wild Warriors were saying horrible stuff about us.'

'So what?' said Jasmine. 'Who are THEY to us? But YOU'RE supposed to be our friend Charlie, and you lied to us. You involved all of us without even asking, then you didn't trust us enough to admit what you'd done. That hurts more than the Wild Warriors calling us names.' She shook her head. 'You'll just have to tell Magpie the bet's off.'

I'd been trying to defend my friends—but all I'd managed to do was make them hate me. When we got back, Magpie would make me stand up in front of everyone and admit that we were rubbish. I could already see the smug look on her face . . .

I couldn't do it!

My friends weren't rubbish, and nobody was going to make me say it.

The flag fluttered in the breeze, taunting me with its nearness. All I had to do was cross the river and wait for the Wild Warriors to turn up. Then I could follow them, steal their flags, and still win the bet.

Simple.

At least it would be if I could find a way across.

I watched the river flow downstream, past a fallen tree reaching out like a giant arm for the opposite bank . . .

My heart kicked.

The tree stopped just a few metres short of the other side. I could jump that!

But what if I fell in?

The current was strong, but would I really get swept away? Jas was just being dramatic.

There might be food supplies with the flag. If I got everyone something to eat, they might even start to forgive me.

Sam and the others were sitting further along the bank with their backs to me. Outback was lying down with his hat over his face.

This was my chance.

I climbed onto the trunk and started edging my way out over the river. The water was noisy, splashing up and making the bark slippery. With every step the tree sagged under my weight, and I had to crouch to keep my balance.

Finally I reached the part of the tree still thick with foliage. I scanned the web of branches and picked a route using the thickest parts. The leaves slapped at my face like hands trying to push me into the river. If I fell in here and got caught up underwater—I would drown.

WOBBLE

I kept going, picturing
the food parcel in my hand, and
the look on my friends' faces when
I handed it to them.

The tree ran out two metres from dry land, but
here the river was shallow enough to wade through.
The cold took my breath away, but didn't stop the
feeling of triumph when I reached the bank.

I looked back and saw Sam, Jas, and Gerbil
watching from the other side. They were waving
their arms and shouting, but I couldn't hear over
the roar of the water. I pointed towards the flag,
then headed into the trees.

When I saw the small plastic bag taped to the flagpole, my hopes of returning with a feast evaporated. I was tempted to look inside, but wanted to get the flag to safety before the Wild Warriors turned up. Having another taken from me would have been too much.

I zipped the mystery package into my tracksuit, and jammed the flag into Adventure Kitten. Then I walked back to the river and waded out. Getting through the top part of the tree was tricky with the flagpole, but I eventually made it onto the trunk.

Outback had now joined the group waiting on the bank—he didn't look happy.

I was halfway back when the tree dipped alarmingly. I looked up and saw Outback climbing on. The idiot was coming to get me!

'GO BACK!' I shouted. 'YOU'RE TOO HEAVY!'

The words had barely left my lips, when there was a crack of splintering wood—and the next thing I knew—I was underwater.

I broke the surface and snatched a gulp of air. There was something tight around my shoulders pulling me down. I imagined slimy fingers of underwater creatures, then realized it was the weight of my own rucksack. I fought my way out, and saw the football spring free from inside. Some deeply rooted instinct kicked in, and I grabbed it.

I clung to the ball while the river swept us downstream. The tree had vanished, but I could see Outback scrambling onto the bank, and the others watching me getting further away with every second.

My fingers
were numb
from the cold
and I was afraid I
would lose my grip
on the ball. I kicked
towards the bank,
but my legs felt
stiff and heavy,
and the current
was too strong.

And then I heard
Survival Clive's voice
in my head.

SOMETIMES IT IS THE PERSON WITH THE STRONGEST WILL, NOT THE GREATEST SKILL, WHO SURVIVES!

I gripped the football and kicked again—
And again—
And again—
Then something smacked into my shoulder, knocking the ball from my hands. I grabbed whatever had hit me, and watched through angry, frustrated tears as the football bobbed away.

I realized I was no longer moving, and looked at the object that had stopped me. It was the flag! It must have floated down and caught on the rocks. I almost laughed.

But I wasn't safe yet. The river was doing its best to tear me free. I needed to get out before my frozen limbs stopped working altogether.

Holding the flagpole for support, I dragged myself along the rocks until my numb feet scraped the river bed, and I could finally crawl onto dry land.

18:36—STRANDED

I'd washed up on the wrong side of the river, miles downstream from the others. The tree was gone,

so they had no way to get across and look for me.
They might think I'd drowned! Outback would
radio base. There would be a search party. Police!
Helicopters! I was going to be in so much trouble
when they found me!

In fact, was that a helicopter coming now?

I strained to listen, then realized the rhythmic
clatter I could hear was actually my own teeth
chattering—in fact, my whole body was shaking.

I needed to make a fire. Get warm. Dry my
clothes. Or there was a danger I could die of . . .
there was a word Survival Clive had used . . . HYPO
. . . something, but my brain was too frozen to
remember. Not important.

FIRE. That was the thing!

I stood there shivering, trying to remember what
to do.

The sparky thing hanging around my neck—
I needed that, but what else?

An image of Magpie's hat flickered into view.
I pushed it away.

155

Come on Charlie, THINK! But my teeth were making such a racket it was hard to concentrate. Burny stuff. That was it . . .

SPARK + BURNY STUFF = FIRE!

I looked around for inspiration, and that was when I noticed the bright orange shape in the rocks at the water's edge. It couldn't be . . .

Adventure Kitten stared up at me with her big scary eyes. Of course THAT had survived—the thing was probably bomb-proof!

I used the flagpole to hook my rucksack from the water, praying there would be something useful left inside. There wasn't—just this notebook, zipped into the pocket.

It was just how Survival Clive had described it on that first morning—all I had was the clothes I was wearing and the things I carried—all of which were soaking wet. I emptied my pockets anyway.

This is what I found:

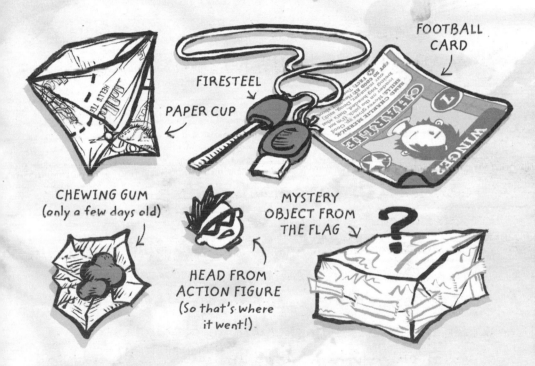

FOOTBALL CARD

FIRESTEEL

PAPER CUP

CHEWING GUM
(only a few days old)

MYSTERY OBJECT FROM THE FLAG

HEAD FROM ACTION FIGURE
(So that's where it went!)

I picked up the thing I'd found strapped to the flag. Hopefully the plastic bag would have protected whatever was inside from the water. I prayed it was something useful—

My numb fingers tore open the bag and a small portable stove landed in my lap.

I felt like crying.

'Fat lot of use that is!' I said out loud.

But I couldn't stop staring at the package. There was something about it that my eyes seemed to be telling me was important.

It was just a box—with a picture of the stove and a warning in big red letters:

CONTENTS FLAMMABLE.

FLAMMABLE said my frozen brain: that means FIRE you idiot!

I clawed at the cardboard, spilling the contents onto the ground. There was a metal tray thing that probably transformed into some clever little cooker. But it was the white blocks wrapped in plastic, and the smell of petrol coming off them, that interested me. FIRE-LIGHTERS! Dad used them to light the barbecue at home. One touch of a match and they would burn for ages. I just had to hope a spark from my firesteel would be enough to get them going.

But first I needed some wood.

I put my few remaining possessions into Adventure Kitten, and stumbled into the trees.

After a while I found a shallow crater, sheltered from the wind. I dropped my pile of sticks on the ground and pulled out the firelighters. My hands were shaking so much I could barely get the firesteel to strike.

I don't think I've ever felt so happy as when that blue flame rolled across the small white block. I piled more cubes on top, then some kindling. For a few minutes there was a lot of smoke but no fire, and I thought it wasn't going to work. Then the first tongues of flame licked along the wood, and I felt heat on my face.

But I was never going to get warm wearing wet clothes. I had to take my things off and dry them by the fire, but what was I supposed to do in the meantime? Stand around naked! Then I saw the flag on the ground. It was made of a shiny material that must have been waterproof, because it was dry already. I tore the cloth off the pole and wrapped it around my waist. It looked like I was wearing a skirt, but there was nobody around to see. Anything was better than standing there in just my pants!

I hung my tracksuit, T-shirt, and socks over a large v-shaped branch and placed it near the fire. Then I propped up the notebook next to it, to dry the pages.

For a moment I almost felt happy, then I remembered the others—the argument, and how much trouble I'd be in when they found me.

19:38—RESCUE?

I was starting to wonder what was taking the rescue party so long, when I heard movement in the trees.

'OVER HERE!' I shouted. 'I'm OVER HERE!'

I waited for an answer, but the forest was suddenly silent.

It was the silence of someone—or someTHING—
listening.

'HELLO?'

Twigs cracked like snapping bones as it moved
through the undergrowth—coming this way.

I grabbed one of the longer sticks from the fire—
still alight at the end. It trailed smoke as I swung it
towards the shape emerging from the trees . . .

FLAG
SKIRT!
↓

'YOU!' I said. 'What are YOU doing here?'

Magpie glared at the flaming stick in my hand.
'I could ask you the same thing,' she said. 'But I'm
more interested in why you're wearing a skirt?'

'It's not a SKIRT, it's a FLAG!' I said. 'And don't
even THINK about taking this one!' I had a horrible
vision of Magpie stealing the flag—leaving me in just
my pants, while her friends stood around laughing.

She shrugged. 'Skirt. Flag. That still doesn't
answer my question.'

I told her what had happened at the river.

Magpie laughed. 'I said you didn't belong here, and you just KEEP ON proving me right!'

'So where are your thieving mates then?' I said. 'Off snaking someone!'

'Listen to you getting down with the lingo! We split up,' she said. 'That way we can collect more flags.'

So that's how they did it.

'You mean ones you don't steal off other people.'

'Survival of the fittest,' said Magpie.

'What about your Observer?'

'Anna? It was her idea. I thought WE were competitive, but she takes it to a whole other level!' Magpie grinned and limped past me.

'What's wrong with your leg?'

She dropped her pack and sat down by the fire. 'I twisted my ankle.'

'Running away after mugging someone, were you?'

'No!' She glanced into the trees. 'There's something out there.'

I snorted. 'Don't bother. I've heard all about the Beast, and the Mutant Sabre-Toothed Squirrel.'

'What are you talking about?' she snapped.
'I'm serious. There's a wild animal in the forest. It chased me.'

'You expect me to fall for that?'

'Don't care! You'll believe it when you're on the end of its tusks!'

'TUSKS?'

She looked at me.

'Was it black? This thing.'

Magpie nodded.

'Sam said he saw something just like that earlier.'

'You see!' said Magpie. 'I TOLD you it was real!'

'What d'you think it is?'

'I don't know,' said Magpie, 'but now it's got our scent, it's probably tracking us.'

20:13—FOOD GLORIOUS FOOD

It was getting dark. I'd expected to be rescued by now, but we hadn't heard a thing. No helicopters, no barking dogs, no voices calling out, just the wind in the trees and the occasional crack of falling branches—at least, that's what I told myself it was.

'They probably think you're dead,' said Magpie. 'They'll call off the search for the body until morning now.'

I was beginning to wonder if they'd even raised the alarm. Maybe Outback and the others were so angry they hadn't bothered to look for me.

'Might as well camp here for the night,' said Magpie, poking at the fire.

I'd been waiting for her to go, but now it was getting dark, I wasn't so keen to be on my own—especially if there WAS a real Beast out there. The fact that Magpie didn't seem to want to leave either made me suspect that she was scared too.

'Got any food?' she said.

'No.'

'We'll have to go foraging then.'

We stacked up the fire so it wouldn't go out while we were gone, then headed off into the trees. Every few metres Magpie stopped to sniff leaves, or peer at berries on a bush.

'What are we looking for exactly?' I said.

'Something we can eat—obviously!'

'Like . . . apples or something?'

Magpie snorted. 'Apples would be nice, yeah—or maybe a toast tree—one with a jam dispenser.' She shook her head. 'This isn't a supermarket you know! We're in a forest! We want edible leaves, mushrooms and berries.'

'Like those?' I pointed to a clump of brambles covered with dark purple fruit.

'Blackberries!' said Magpie.

She limped over to the bush and started shoving fistfuls into her mouth. The juice ran down her chin and made her look like a vampire.

'Shouldn't we wash them first, or something?' I said.

Magpie spat out a laugh. 'Yeah, we'll take them back and wash them under the tap shall we?' She shook her head. 'You are SUCH a city boy! If you want to eat tonight I suggest you start picking.'

We filled Adventure Kitten with as many blackberries as we could reach, then moved on.

TOAST TREE

JAM

I felt quite pleased with myself. It had been me—the CITY BOY—who had found the blackberry bush, not Magpie the great Wild Warrior. She knew it too, which was probably why she insisted on hunting for some mushrooms.

'I hate mushrooms,' I said.

'Don't care. Bet you've never even tasted WILD mushrooms, have you?'

'No, but if they taste like the tame ones, I won't like them.'

After another ten minutes trampling through the undergrowth, Magpie let out a small cry of triumph and crouched down next to a tree stump. There was a ring of yellow fungus growing round it.

'You're not seriously going to eat that!' I said.

Magpie gave me a pitying look. 'They're Chanterelles, you idiot. Delicious!'

As far as I was concerned ALL mushrooms were evil, and in the dim light of the forest, the ones Magpie was picking seemed to be giving off an eerie radioactive glow.

✳

'Pity we don't have any butter,' said Magpie, when we got back to camp. 'These are delicious sautéed in oil.' Which didn't sound like a very Wild Warrior thing to say.

You could tell the mushrooms were disgusting, but Magpie ate them anyway—just to prove she was some great foraging expert who could survive in the wild better than me. But it was me who had got our fire going, and me who found the blackberries.

In fact, the more I thought about it, ever since I'd been in a REAL SURVIVAL SITUATION, and not just taking part in some stupid FIND THE FLAG game, I'd been doing OK. Even my paper cup had come in handy when Magpie had begrudgingly agreed to let me have some of her water.

EERIE GLOW

As darkness closed in around us, Magpie rigged up a tarp shelter. We agreed to take turns to keep watch and make sure the fire didn't go out.

My tracksuit had dried enough to put back on, but I kept the flag under my t-shirt—I didn't trust Magpie not to steal it and disappear while I slept. She clearly felt the same, and lay down with the three flags she had, clasped in her arms.

I volunteered to take the first watch.

'D'you think the fire will keep the Beast away?' I said.

Magpie looked up at me. 'Depends how hungry it is.' She shrugged. 'Anyway, I'm hoping if we stick together, there's a fifty-fifty chance whatever is out there will eat you first!'

Oddly enough, I'd been thinking exactly the same thing myself!

03:42
NIGHT
WATCH

i KNEW SOMETHING WAS WRONG THE MOMENT i WOKE UP . . .

i PEERED OUT FROM UNDER THE SHELTER AND LISTENED.

SILENCE. WHERE WAS MAGPIE?

SHE'D LET THE FIRE GO OUT!

ABANDONED ME WHILE I WAS SLEEPING!

BUT HER RUCKSACK AND FLAGS WERE STILL HERE.

FLAGS!!!

THIS WAS EXACTLY WHAT i'D PLANNED!

TAKE THE FLAGS AND WIN THE GAME!

i SHOULD GO NOW. DISAPPEAR INTO THE TREES BEFORE SHE CAME BACK.

BUT WHAT ABOUT THE **BEAST?**

THE BEAST WAS JUST A STORY. iT WASN'T REAL . . . **WAS iT?**

'Put those down!'

I jumped as Magpie materialized from the shadows.

'You let the fire go out!' I said, keeping hold of the flags while I picked up Adventure Kitten.

I wondered if Magpie would be able to chase me with her bad ankle.

'I told you to put those down!' she growled.

'You want them. Come and get them!'

Magpie made a lurch towards me, then stumbled and crashed to the ground. This was my chance to make a run for it while she was down. If I was quick, she wouldn't even see which direction I'd gone.

So why wasn't I moving?

Because Magpie . . . was CRYING!

This wasn't the Magpie I knew and loathed. What was wrong with her?

It wasn't my problem. I needed to GO.

But I couldn't.

I sighed and walked over to her. 'What's wrong?'

Magpie lifted her head and looked at me, then her face creased—and she threw up.

I jumped out of the way just in time.

Great! What was I supposed to do now? A weeping, vomiting girl would have been hard enough to deal with in normal circumstances, but in the middle of the night, alone in a forest . . . I tried to remember what mum did when I was sick.

'D'you want some water?'

Magpie nodded.

'I bet it was those mushrooms,' I said. 'I told you they were evil!'

In Survival Clive's WILD FOOD slideshow, there had been one slide that had made everyone sit up.

THERE IS NO CURE FOR POISONING FROM CERTAIN MUSHROOMS.

YOU WILL DIE!

I found
Magpie's head-torch
and opened my notebook.
Apart from crinkly edges
and a few smudges, it seemed to
have dried out OK, but I couldn't
find a section entitled: WHAT TO DO
IF YOU FIND YOURSELF ALONE IN A
FOREST WITH A GIRL WHO WAS DUMB
ENOUGH TO EAT A LOAD OF POISONED
MUSHROOMS.

I did however find my notes on the
CHANTERELLE mushroom, and suddenly
everything became horribly clear.

CHANTERELLE
(CANTHARELLUS CIBARIUS)
COLOUR: EGG YELLOW
FOUND: WOODLAND
SEASON: SUMMER-AUTUMN
EDIBLE: YES

BEWARE THE FALSE CHANTERELLE
OR **JACK O'LANTERN**
VERY SIMILAR IN APPEARANCE AND
LOCATION TO REAL CHANTERELLE,
BUT POISONOUS TO HUMANS!
THE JACK O'LANTERN CAN BE
DISTINGUISHED BY THE FACT IT
GLOWS IN THE DARK—
THE PROPERTY WHICH EARNS THE
MUSHROOM ITS NAME.

Magpie had eaten Jack O'Lanterns which were poisonous to humans! Did that mean she could DIE?

I needed to get help—

But how?

Somewhere with a telephone, or a vehicle . . .

An image of the Frankenbus rolled into my mind. Right now it would be parked outside the Go! Wild Centre.

That was my best hope. Find my way back to base.

But how far was that? And which way?

Magpie's compass and map were in the side-pocket of her pack, but I had no idea how to use them to work out our current position. It was hopeless! Magpie was going to die just because I couldn't read a map!

COME ON CHARLIE! You're the only hope she has. THINK!

On the first day Jasmine had said that the Go! Wild Centre was north of us. I didn't know how far we'd moved since then, but north seemed like a good direction to try.

IF YOU KEEP WALKING ON THE SAME **BEARING** YOU WILL EVENTUALLY ARRIVE SOMEWHERE!

SURVIVAL TIP

But walking anywhere required Magpie getting up off the ground, and she wasn't into that idea AT ALL!

I knelt down out of vomit range. 'Magpie! You have to get up.'

'Stomach hurts,' she said

'Come on!' I held out my hand. She scowled, and for a moment I saw a glimpse of the old Magpie, then her fingers closed around mine and I pulled her up. She moaned and clutched her belly, but stayed on her feet.

I handed Magpie the flagpole to use as a walking stick, then picked up Adventure Kitten and the other flags—then we headed out.

05:32—BLUE UNICORNS

The sky above the canopy was starting to lighten, and I could see further into the trees. I could also see how bad Magpie looked. Her face was shiny with sweat, and I was struggling to hold her up while she stumbled along, making weird wheezing sounds and moaning about how much her stomach hurt.

But the thing that really worried me was the fact that we might be walking in the WRONG DIRECTION. For all I knew, the Go! Wild Centre could be ten minutes off to our right!

When we staggered into a clearing filled with sculptures of giant wooden mushrooms, it was ALMOST funny . . .

Magpie stopped suddenly and pointed into the forest. 'Look!'

For a moment I thought she'd seen somebody —a path or a signpost— something useful . . . but there was nothing there.

180

'Blue unicorn!' said Magpie, staring into thin air.

I realized the poison from the mushrooms was making her see things. I saw a film once where the same thing happened . . . it didn't end well.

'Blue unicorns like ice-cream,' said Magpie, sliding to the ground.

I dragged her back into a standing position, but the second I let go, she fell down again.

An hour later, we stumbled into another clearing filled with more wooden mushrooms!

'You're kidding,' I said.

Except it wasn't MORE mushrooms, it was the SAME mushrooms, and the SAME clearing. We'd gone in a complete circle.

I could have wept. My body ached from all the dragging and pushing and carrying, and we were still no closer to base.

'The blue unicorn lives here,' said Magpie, as fat drops of rain started slapping against the leaves.

I scowled at the sky. 'Seriously?'

But the cold rain seemed to shock Magpie back to reality. 'Where are we?' she grunted.

'I dunno.' I frowned at the map, but it was pointless. The squiggles and symbols bore no resemblance to anything around me. If only they'd marked the sculptures on the map, then I'd know where we were.

Magpie demanded water, and when I passed her the bottle, something sparked in my brain.

My paper cup! I'd made it from a leaflet about the sculpture trail—there might be a map!

Sure enough, when I carefully unfolded the cup, there it was—wrinkled, torn and faded, but still perfectly legible.

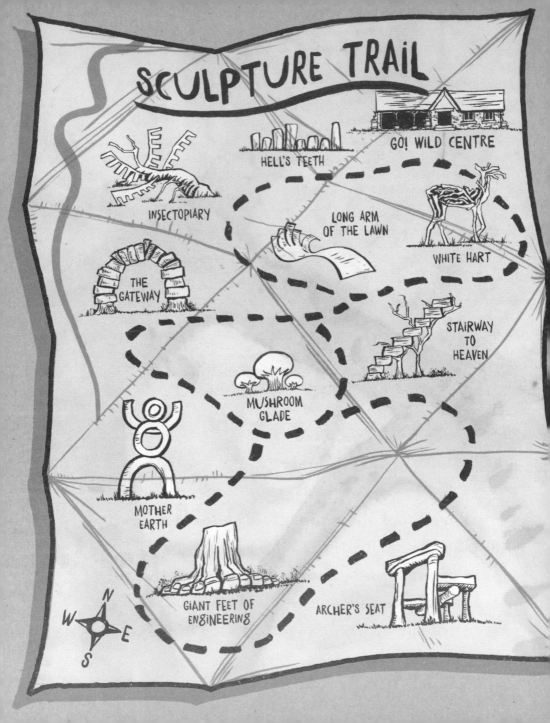

Here were the mushrooms! And there was the Go! Wild Centre—and a trail of sculptures leading all the way from here to there!

I'd done it! I'd found a way to get us back.

I lined up the compass and worked out which direction we needed to get to the next sculpture, then dragged Magpie to her feet.

'Come on,' I said. 'We're going home!'

07:03—SOME SINGING AND SOME SHOUTING

Magpie was shuffling along like a zombie, and the rain wasn't helping. My arm ached from trying to keep her upright. If she lost consciousness completely we'd be finished. I had to find a way to keep her awake.

'How about a song?' I said.

Magpie didn't answer.

'I've got one—I don't know but I've been told!'

I cringed at the sound of my voice, but kept going. 'Then you say—Warriors smell like foot-cheese mould!' Even in Magpie's current condition, this was like teasing a bear. 'We can change the words if you like,' I said. 'How about—

I DON'T KNOW BUT I'VE BEEN TOLD,
CHANTERELLE MUSHROOMS LOOK LiKE GOLD.
i DON'T KNOW BUT IT'S BEEN SAiD.
JACK O'LANTERNS KiLL YOU DEAD . . .

No, you're right. Maybe not.'

By the time we reached the next sculpture, the rain had stopped, but my optimism was draining away. The downside of knowing where we were, was being able to see how much further we still had to go. I was exhausted, and Magpie's breathing was getting worse with each stumbling step.

'Look!' she pointed behind me with a shaky hand.

'Blue unicorn come back has he?' I said, trying to keep the compass still enough to get a reading.

'CHARLIE!' said Magpie.

Hearing her use my name was enough of a shock to make me look up. Then I noticed her eyes—unusually clear and focussed—staring at something over my shoulder.

A cold dread shivered down my spine as I turned around . . .

The Beast stood at the edge of the trees. It was the size of a large dog, and it was staring right at us.

The creature's body was covered in coarse black fur. Its tusks gleamed in the sunlight, sharp and slightly curved, sprouting either side of the broad flat jaw.

'I told you it was real,' croaked Magpie.

'Don't move,' I whispered. 'It might just go away.'

Which is when the Beast snorted—and charged towards us.

I decided it might be wise to follow its example, and set off in the opposite direction.

I'd gone three metres before I realized Magpie hadn't come with me. She was still slumped against the sculpture, while a hundred kilos of muscle and tusk hurtled towards her.

I skidded to a halt, pulled one of the flags from the rucksack, then ran back, waving the pole in front of me and yelling—partly to scare the Beast, but mainly because it sounded better than the high-pitched scream that was trying to escape from my throat.

For a few seconds we played a bizarre game of CHICKEN . . .

Realizing that the Beast was not some mutant monster, but a real live wild pig, didn't change the fact that it was huge and about to crash into me.

I was seriously starting to question the wisdom of my actions, when the Beast changed direction and veered off into the trees. I watched it disappear, then realized I was still shouting. I closed my mouth, but strangely the sound carried on—except now it was calling my name.

I turned round just in time to see Sam burst through the trees with his spear, closely followed by Jasmine, Gerbil, and Outback.

'It's gone!' I said.

'What?' said Sam.

'The Beast!'

'What Beast?' said Gerbil.

'Don't tell me you didn't see it! Ask Magpie.'

'MAGPIE! What's SHE doing here?' said Sam. 'And what's wrong with her?'

Magpie's eyes had gone glassy again, and the only thing she wanted to talk about was blue unicorns.

I explained about the mushrooms.

'You have to call base,' I said to Outback. 'We need a helicopter or something to come and get her.'

Jasmine shook her head. 'He lost his radio when he fell in the river.'

'We're going to have to do it on foot and carry her,' said Outback. 'It's about two hours to base from here. Ninety minutes if we get a move on!'

'Will she last that long?' said Jasmine.

Outback lifted Magpie and slung her over his shoulder— but didn't answer the question.

We jogged most of the way, walking every so often to get our breath back. Magpie slipped in and out of consciousness. Nobody said much. We all thought she was going to die.

Finally, we broke through the trees and ran down the slope towards the Go! Wild Centre.

Survival Clive and Doug came out to meet us, and then everything seemed to happen all at once. People rushing round. Sirens and paramedics. I lost count of how many times I had to describe the mushrooms that Magpie had eaten.

Then they took her away in an ambulance, and it wasn't until the sound of the siren finally stopped bouncing off the hills that I realized everyone was staring at me.

'What?'

'You know you saved her life,' Outback said.

'But Survival Clive reckoned those mushrooms weren't the sort that kill you,' I reminded him.

'No, but if she'd have been on her own when she got sick, who knows what might have happened.'

I shrugged. 'I couldn't just leave her.'

'I would've!' said Sam. But he didn't mean it. Sam had run all the way back in flip-flops and never moaned once.

'I'm proud of you, Charlie,' said Jasmine.

'I thought you'd still be mad at me.'

'Oh, I am,' she said, 'furious! But I can't let people see me being mean to the hero can I?'

'Yeah,' said Sam. 'We're only hanging out with you because it makes us look good. We're not really mates anymore.'

'We hate you,' said Gerbil, then he frowned and whispered to Sam. 'We are joking, aren't we?'

Outback sighed. 'I'm not joking. I'm in serious trouble because of you, Charlie Merrick!'

'Why? You carried Magpie all the way back. I could never have done that!'

'Survival Clive's still gonna chew me out for not stopping you from crossing that river, AND losing my radio. My only job was to keep you safe, and I nearly got us both killed!'

'Yeah, but if Charlie hadn't fallen in the river, he wouldn't have been there to save Magpie,' said Gerbil. 'So, it's lucky you didn't do your job properly!'

Outback laughed. 'Thanks Gerb—I think!'

'You fell in the river?' said Doug, who was always a bit slow to catch up.

'It's a long story,' I said. 'When I've finished writing it down you can read all about it.' I pulled my notebook from Adventure Kitten and wiped off the smears of blackberry juice, mud and ash.

'You've still got that!' said Jasmine.

'Yep, it's the only thing I didn't lose in the river.' I tapped the book and grinned. 'It's all in here. Except I don't know what happened to you lot after I got washed away.'

'Well,' said Gerbil. 'Jas climbed a tree and saw you get out of the river, but then you disappeared into the forest. We had to walk miles before we found somewhere to cross. We were looking for you all night!'

'Thanks,' I said.

'Thanks?' said Jasmine. 'Is that it?'

'And . . . sorry.' I shrugged. 'For everything.'

'So you should be,' she said, then hugged me. After a moment Sam and Gerbil joined in.

'You got WASHED AWAY?' said Doug.

We were still sitting outside when the other squads started appearing over the crest of the hill, like aircraft returning from a mission. The Fireflies were first, followed soon after by the Wild Warriors.

'I wonder if Anna knows how much trouble she's in,' said Outback. 'Survival Clive almost popped his glass eye out when he heard she'd sent the Warriors off on their own collecting flags!'

197

Finally, as the giant egg-yolk sun slid towards the horizon, the Forest Freaks rolled out of the trees. It felt like a lifetime had passed since I'd seen Kash, Nathan, Oscar, and Donut.

We ran up the field to meet them.

Sam told them what had happened to us, so then I had to tell the whole story. When I got to the part about fighting off the Beast, Oscar stopped me.

'It must have been a wild pig,' he said. 'We saw a whole family of them!'

I blushed. In my dramatic account of the incident, I'd neglected to mention the fact that I'd realized the creature was more BACON than BEAST!

'A PIG!' said Jas, starting to laugh.

'A WILD one,' I reminded her. 'With TUSKS!'

'Still a pig though!'

They all started making jokes then, about me chasing pigs with flags, but I didn't mind. It was just good to see everyone again.

I forgot all about the bet, until Survival Clive posted the final positions on the leader board.

WILD WARRIORS 51

FIREFLIES 43

FOREST FREAKS 36

MISFITS 30

'I thought they'd give you extra points for being a hero and saving Magpie,' said Gerbil. 'Like they do in Harry Potter!'

'And pig-jousting,' said Jasmine. 'We should have got something for that!'

'Ha! Ha!' I said. 'You . . .' Then I saw Hawk walking towards us. This was it—she was going to call in the bet. I would have to stand up in front of everyone and announce that my friends were rubbish—a joke—and didn't deserve to be here. Or, we would all have to do the Leap of Doom, which the others had already told me in no uncertain terms, wasn't going to happen.

But Hawk just thanked me for saving Magpie, and didn't mention the bet. I was starting to wonder if Magpie had even told them about it. Maybe everything was going to work out after all.

21:38—THE BONFiRE TREATY

It was a Go! Wild tradition to end the week with a bonfire party. Everyone sat round toasting marshmallows and eating hot dogs, while Gerbil and Outback made up songs—until Hawk threatened to throw them both, and the guitar, on the fire.

Sam came back from the barbecue clutching a hot-dog in each hand. 'I couldn't choose between mustard or ketchup. So . . .' He paused mid-sentence, his eyes widening in surprise.

When I turned around, Magpie was standing behind me, wrapped up in a huge coat. Even in the glow from the fire, her face looked pale.

'I thought you were in hospital,' I said.

'They let me out.'

'So, you're OK then?'

She nodded, then frowned. 'They said if I'd been on my own, I might have died.'

'That's right,' said Jas. 'Charlie saved your life!'

'He's a hero,' said Sam.

Magpie looked at them, then back at me. 'Thanks.'

'Thanks?' Sam said. 'Is that it?'

'Thanks is fine,' I said quickly, before Sam suggested Magpie should hug me. I steered her away from the others. 'About that other thing.'

'It's OK, you don't have to do it,' said Magpie. 'I still won though.'

'You think so?'

She snorted. 'Duh! Misfits came last!'

'Who cares about the stupid leader board,' I said. 'I only made the bet to prove that you were wrong about my friends being useless. But in the end I didn't have to. They proved it themselves.'

'How d'you work that out?' said Magpie.
'Your squad got the lowest points total ever!
They're a joke, just like I said.'

I sighed. 'You still don't get it, do you?'

'What?'

'This week wasn't about FLAG
COLLECTING! It was about survival.'

'So?'

'So—when I fell in the river, my
friends walked miles looking for
me. It was MY friends who found us,
and got YOU to hospital. What were
your friends doing at the time?'

'They didn't know I was ill,'
said Magpie.

'Because they'd sent you off
collecting flags on your own!'

She frowned. 'Is there a POINT to this?'

'The point is—we made a bet because you said
my friends were useless. I'm saying they proved
you wrong when they saved us both.'

Magpie looked at me, then gave a sneer. 'Your lot would have been too chicken to do the Leap of Doom anyway!'

'No, we wouldn't!'

'Prove it,' said Magpie.

I laughed. 'I'm not making any more bets.'

'No bet, just me and you,' she said. 'We'll do it together.'

'The Leap of Doom?'

She nodded, and her eyes flashed a fiery orange.

I shrugged, then heard a voice that sounded horribly like mine say: 'OK.' Which was ridiculous, because why would I agree to something like that?

But apparently I had, because Magpie gave a mean grin and said: 'Half six tomorrow morning then—Devil Falls. Make sure nobody sees you leave the centre.'

06:23—DEVIL FALLS

I climbed the hill into the forest and followed the path to DEVIL FALLS, shaking my head in disbelief. Only I could have talked myself into something as stupid as this! I was shivering — my legs felt like someone had taken out the bones during the night and filled the space with cold custard.

I clung to the hope that Magpie wouldn't be there, but when I reached the top, the Wild Warriors were waiting. I wished Sam, Jas, and Gerbil had come with me, but if I'd told them what I was going to do, they would have stopped it.

'Didn't think you'd show,' said Magpie.

'Are you kidding?' I said. 'Wouldn't have missed this for anything!' I forced a grin and peered over the edge.

There was no point delaying. Better to get it over with before I lost my nerve.

I sat down on the grass to take off my trainers.

'Make sure you get a good leap out into the middle,' said Owl. 'So you don't hit anything on the way down.' She sounded nervous—and SHE wasn't even doing the jump!

I stood up. The grass felt cold under my bare feet. WHAT WAS I DOING?

'So, we're going at the same time, yeah?' I said, trying to hide the wobble in my voice.

Magpie nodded. She looked as scared as me!

'We'll count you down,' said Falcon, as we walked back from the edge to give ourselves a run-up.

'FIVE!' shouted the Wild Warriors.
It was like waiting to take a penalty.
'FOUR!'
No time to think.
'THREE!'
Just focus—
'TWO!'
And
. . .

'STOP!'

I rocked on my toes, and stared at Magpie.

'I can't do it,' she said, sitting down on the grass and lowering her head into her hands.

The Wild Warriors gasped, but before anyone could say anything, we heard voices in the trees.

I turned, and saw Jasmine, Sam, Gerbil, and Outback running towards us.

'What are you doing here?' I said, though I'd never been more pleased to see them in my life.

'Outback saw you sneak out and guessed what you were up to,' said Sam. 'So he came and got us.'

'Sorry, Charlie,' said Outback. 'But if you're going to do this, I can't let you jump without the proper safety gear.'

He unzipped the large bag he was carrying and handed me a life jacket and a helmet.

'Don't worry,' I said. 'Magpie just called it off!'

'What? You mean I've been dragged out of bed and run all the way up here for nothing!' said Sam.

'Not necessarily.' Jasmine took the helmet from Outback. 'This looks like fun.'

'YOU'RE going to do the Leap of Doom!' said Gerbil, his eyes bulging.

Jasmine shrugged. 'I've always wanted to do a cliff jump.'

'But you said . . .' I stared at her.

'I was annoyed because you didn't ASK.' Jas grinned, then flicked her eyes towards the Wild Warriors, who were staring with their mouths open. 'So—you coming, Charlie?'

I swallowed, then nodded.

'Me too,' said Gerbil.

Outback laughed. 'Seeing as how I'm supposed to be keeping an eye on you, I'd better come as well!'

Sam had gone very pale, but then he reached into the bag and pulled out a helmet.

'What?' he said. 'You think I'm going to let you lot do this on your own?'

It's hard to describe how I felt at that moment—happy that I had the best mates in the world, and at the same time, absolutely terrified. The look on the Wild Warriors' faces was hilarious. The mocking sneers were gone. They finally understood that the Misfits, for all our failings, were proper friends who would always be there to back each other up.

'Start the countdown when you're ready,' I said.

This time when the Wild Warriors called out 'ONE!' we grabbed each other's hands, and ran towards the edge . . .

STAYING ALIVE WITH SURVIVAL CLIVE

DON'T FORGET—UNLESS YOU ARE DIVING WITH QUALIFIED INSTRUCTORS, AND THE CORRECT SAFETY EQUIPMENT, YOU SHOULD NEVER JUMP INTO WATER. THERE MIGHT BE ROCKS AND OTHER OBSTACLES HIDDEN BELOW THE SURFACE THAT COULD CAUSE INJURY OR ENTANGLEMENT.

PLEASE NOTE: THE SURVIVAL TIPS AND INFORMATION INCLUDED IN THIS BOOK ARE ACCURATE TO THE BEST OF THE AUTHOR'S KNOWLEDGE. HOWEVER, THIS IS A WORK OF FICTION—NOT A SURVIVAL GUIDE! FOR ANYONE WISHING TO LEARN BUSHCRAFT AND SURVIVAL TECHNIQUES THERE ARE MANY COURSES AND BOOKS AVAILABLE OFFERING EXPERT ADVICE AND TRAINING.

AUTHOR

DAVE

Name: DAVE COUSINS
Skills: SCRIBBLING WORDS AND PICTURES.
WILD FACT: ONCE FOUND HIMSELF STRANDED AND WAS FORCED TO SURVIVE A NIGHT ALONE WITH NO FOOD OR WATER, SHELTERING IN A RED TELEPHONE BOX!

ABANDONING CHILDHOOD PLANS TO BE AN ASTRONAUT, DAVE COUSINS HITCHED A RIDE WITH A TRAVELLING CIRCUS AND BECAME A ROCK STAR (ALMOST). THE FIRST STORIES HE WROTE WERE FOR HIS OWN COMIC—ABOUT A FOOTBALL TEAM AND A SUPERHERO MOUSE WITH A ROCKET POWERED CAR!

AS WELL AS WRITING AND DRAWING THE CHARLIE MERRICK STORIES, DAVE HAS WRITTEN A NUMBER OF AWARD-WINNING BOOKS FOR TEENAGERS. *15 DAYS WITHOUT A HEAD* HAS BEEN PUBLISHED IN OVER TEN LANGUAGES ACROSS THE WORLD, AND *WAITING FOR GONZO* HAS ITS OWN MUSIC SOUNDTRACK! (VISIT WWW.DAVECOUSINS.NET TO DOWNLOAD THE ALBUM & WATCH THE VIDEOS.)

WHEN NOT SCRIBBLING STORIES OR PLAYING SUBBUTEO WITH THE CAT, DAVE SPENDS HIS TIME VISITING SCHOOLS, LIBRARIES AND BOOK FESTIVALS.

KEEP UP TO DATE WITH DAVE, CHARLIE & THE MISFITS AT WWW.DAVECOUSINS.NET

🅑 @DAVECOUSINS9000   🅕 FACEBOOK.COM/DAVECOUSINSAUTHOR

THANK YOU

NEIL ARMSTRONG IS FAMOUS FOR BEING THE FIRST PERSON TO SET FOOT ON THE MOON, BUT ARMSTRONG WOULDN'T HAVE MADE IT INTO SPACE WITHOUT A LOT OF HELP. PRODUCING THE BOOK YOU ARE NOW HOLDING, MAY NOT HAVE REQUIRED A KNOWLEDGE OF ROCKET SCIENCE, BUT IT ONLY EXISTS THANKS TO THE HARD WORK OF A TEAM OF VERY CLEVER AND DEDICATED PEOPLE, TO WHOM I WOULD LIKE TO GIVE THANKS . . .

IT ACTUALLY TAKES LONGER TO WRITE AND DRAW A BOOK THAN IT DOES TO FLY TO THE MOON! I WOULD NOT HAVE LASTED THE DISTANCE WITHOUT THE SUPPORT OF MY FAMILY AND FRIENDS—TOO MANY TO MENTION BY NAME HERE, BUT YOU KNOW WHO YOU ARE! SPECIAL THANKS TO JANE FOR ACCOMPANYING ME TO THE WOODS TO TRY OUT MY SURVIVAL SKILLS AND NOT LAUGHING TOO HARD AT MY FAILED ATTEMPTS TO BUILD A TARP SHELTER. GRATITUDE TO DYLAN FOR HIS PATIENCE POSING FOR ACTION STANCES I HAD TO DRAW, AND TO PTOL AND HOCK FOR INSPIRATION (AND OUTBACK!).

WITHOUT THE SUPPORT AND GUIDANCE OF THE MARVELLOUS TEAM AT OXFORD UNIVERSITY PRESS MISSION CONTROL, THIS BOOK WOULD NEVER HAVE LEFT THE LAUNCHPAD. HUGE THANKS TO EVERYONE IN EDITORIAL, PUBLICITY & MARKETING, SALES AND FOREIGN-RIGHTS, BUT ESPECIALLY CLARE WHITSTON AND CLAIRE WESTWOOD, FOR HELPING ME PLOT THE ROUTE, AND TO KAREN STEWART FOR HER TRUST AND SKILLS IN MAKING SURE I HAD THE MAP THE RIGHT WAY UP! MY AGENT, JENNY SAVILL, PROVIDED VALUABLE WORDS OF WISDOM WHEN THIS STORY WAS JUST SCRIBBLES IN MY NOTEBOOK—THANKS JENNY AND SORRY THE GOAT DIDN'T MAKE THE FINAL CUT!

FINALLY THANKS TO ALL THE LIBRARIANS, TEACHERS, BOOKSELLERS, FESTIVAL ORGANISERS AND REVIEWERS, WITHOUT WHOM MY STORIES WOULD NEVER FIND THEIR WAY TO READERS—A MUCH MORE IMPORTANT DESTINATION THAN THE MOON (IN MY OPINION).

READ ON FOR MORE CHARLIE MERRICK ACTION!

NORTH ★ GALAXY

UNDER—12s

FOOTBALL—it's all I ever think about. I dream about it when I'm asleep. At school I'm always getting told off for doodling kits and formations. My art teacher says I've got REAL TALENT— I just need to widen my subject matter. So I drew all the away kits to go with the home ones. She wasn't impressed.

WINGER

7

★

CHARLIE

NAME: CHARLIE MERRICK
SKILLS: Never gives up. Good leader on the pitch. (I'm not being big-headed, that's what our manager, Doug, said!)
NOT SO GOOD AT: Heading; shooting.
★ **FACT:** Team Captain.

I wish my real talent was football. I can always see the pass or when to make a run into space. The PROBLEM comes when I get the ball. That's when my FEET need to take over. The trouble is, they're NOT QUITE AS GOOD

AT FOOTBALL as my BRAIN!

This is my first season as
captain of NORTH STAR GALAXY
UNDER-12s. All our best players left
to join another club, so it's just the subs
and the people nobody else wanted in the team now.
My best mate Sam calls us CHARLIE MERRICK'S
MISFITS—which is about right really!

I'm going to tell you everything that happens—the
TRUTH—however painful that might be. I don't
know how it's going to end. By the time I finish
writing and you finish reading . . . we'll both know!

Charlie Merrick

(team captain)

North Star Galaxy
v
Cedar Street Wasps

There's losing and then there's LOSING! Getting TROUNCED. BATTERED. HUMILIATED.

Five games. Five defeats. You'd think we'd be used to it by now . . .

'Eleven—nil!' said Donut. 'ELEVEN!'

'NIL!!' added Gerbil, in case he'd forgotten.

'Remember lads, football's not just about winning,' said Doug, our manager.

Sam scowled. 'I thought that was the whole point!'

'Well, that's certainly the aim.' Doug scratched his beard. 'I'd say the POINT is the pure pleasure of playing the beautiful game!'

If Doug thinks THAT was beautiful, he must have been watching with his eyes shut.

'How can anyone enjoy losing eleven—nil?' I muttered.

'You want to try being in goal!' said Sam. 'I've never lost count of how many I let in before.'

Jasmine laughed. 'Well, you have only got ten fingers!'

She's allowed to say stuff like that, because every week Jasmine stands on the touchline . . . and watches us lose.

'Right then lads, gather round,' said Doug.

Sam rolled his eyes. 'Here comes the speech.'

No.1 FAN

1

JASMINE

NAME: JASMINE LAWRENCE
SKILLS: Mind Control (Jas can make you do what she wants).
NOT SO GOOD AT: Jas is perfect (see).
⭐ FACT: Me, Sam, & Jas have been friends since Reception, but we're still a bit scared of her!

GOALKEEPER

13

SAM

NAME: SAMSON CHARSLEY
(Seriously! His mum's a bit weird.)
SKILLS: Has no fear!
NOT SO GOOD AT: Corners and high shots. Very small for a goalie.
⭐ FACT: Sleeps in his lucky No. 13 shirt the night before every match.

'Hang on, I just need my phone,' I said, digging into my bag.

Doug frowned. 'Do you have to record this, Charlie?'

'It's for the World Cup competition. I need to write down everything that happens. I'll have forgotten what you said by the time I get home!'

SUPER SUB

12

GERBIL

NAME: **CIARAN MORGAN**
SKILLS: Never stops smiling.
NOT SO GOOD AT: Football.
⭐ FACT: Gerbil has never scored a goal, even in training. When he misses, Gerb shrugs & says 'one day'. That day is yet to arrive . . .

'You're not still planning to send that in are you?' said Donut. 'We'll never get picked to play at the World Cup if we get thrashed eleven—nil every week!'

'It was only nine last week,' said Gerbil.

Donut snorted.

'Anyway,' I said. 'The history of football is full of teams doing incredible things against the odds, so why not North Star?'

STATMAN ☆ FACT

IN 1996, A TEAM FROM **ITALY** CALLED *CASTEL DI SANGRO* WERE PROMOTED TO SERIE B. THEY HAD CLIMBED ALL THE WAY FROM THE LOWEST AMATEUR LEAGUES TO PLAY ALONGSIDE SOME OF THE BIGGEST NAMES IN ITALIAN FOOTBALL. **THE NEWSPAPERS CALLED IT A MIRACLE!**

BOOKS FOR TEENS, BY DAVE COUSINS.

HOW FAR WOULD YOU GO TO KEEP YOUR FAMILY TOGETHER?

MEET LAURENCE—FIFTEEN YEARS OLD AND SIX FEET TALL—HE'LL DRESS UP AS HIS MUM AND IMPERSONATE A DEAD MAN ON THE RADIO.

MEET JAY—HIS SIX YEAR OLD BROTHER. HE LOOKS LIKE AN ANGEL BUT THINKS HE'S A DOG. HE'LL SINK HIS TEETH INTO ANYONE WHO GETS IN THE WAY.

TODAY IS TUESDAY—AND THE NEXT FIFTEEN DAYS WILL CHANGE THE BOYS' LIVES FOR EVER . . .

DAVE COUSINS
15 DAYS WITHOUT A HEAD

A tough and turbulent ... There's ... ... page.

WAITING FOR GONZO

Anyone can make a MISTAKE. To mess things up BIG TIME takes real GENIUS

OZ HAS A TALENT FOR TROUBLE, BUT HIS HEART'S IN THE RIGHT PLACE . . . USUALLY.

WHEN A JOKE BACKFIRES ON THE FIRST DAY AT HIS NEW SCHOOL, OZ ATTRACTS THE ATTENTION OF ISOBEL SKINNER—THE TOUGHEST KID IN YEAR 9. HIS OLDER SISTER'S NO HELP, BUT THEN SHE'S GOT A PROBLEM OF HER OWN—ONE THAT'S GROWING BIGGER BY THE DAY.

OZ KNOWS HE'S GOT TO PUT THINGS RIGHT, BUT LIFE ISN'T THAT SIMPLE—ESPECIALLY WHEN THE ONLY PEOPLE STILL TALKING TO YOU ARE A HOBBIT-OBSESSED GEEK AND A VOICE IN YOUR OWN HEAD!